A FATE TOTALLY
WORSE THAN DEATH

Paul Fleischman is one of America's leading writers of fiction for young people. "As a teenager," he says, "I loved humour that mocked the adult world. As a writer, I found little humour in young adult books. Teenage horror novels seemed especially ripe for parody." And so was born *A Fate Totally Worse than Death*. The author has won numerous awards, including the Newbery Medal for *Joyful Noise: Poems for Two Voices*, and his picture book *Weslandia* was Commended for the Kate Greenaway Medal. Paul makes his home in California.

A Fate Totally Worse Than Death

Paul Fleischman

WALKER BOOKS
AND SUBSIDIARIES
LONDON · BOSTON · SYDNEY · AUCKLAND

For Amy and Kate
– *Paul*

First published in Great Britain 1996
by Walker Books Ltd,
87 Vauxhall Walk, London SE11 5HJ

2 4 6 8 10 9 7 5 3 1

Text © 1995 Paul Fleischman
Cover illustration by Phil Schramm

The right of Paul Fleischman to be identified as author
of this work has been asserted by him in accordance
with the Copyright, Designs and Patents Act 1988

This book has been typeset in Sabon

Printed in Great Britain
by Cox & Wyman Ltd, Reading, Berkshire

British Library Cataloguing in Publication Data:
a catalogue record for this book is available
from the British Library

ISBN 1-84428-608-8

www.walkerbooks.co.uk

CHAPTER ONE

Danielle despised waiting in lines. Mixing body mechanics and brazen gall, she edged past a bent-backed, blind woman and her dog, then two tottering veterans of San Juan Hill, then a mother with triplets, and squeezed onto the bus. She saw the sign above the seat reserving it for senior citizens. She also saw that it was the last seat left. She grabbed it, pretending not to notice the parade of the old and infirm shuffling past. Last to board, the blind woman halted directly before her and groped for a handhold. Just my luck, thought Danielle. Helen Keller has to stop next to *me*. She felt poison-tipped glances thrust at her by her neighbours. The Whistler's Mother look-alike to her left cleared her throat in a meaningful fashion. Danielle rolled her eyes, unzipped her pack, pulled out *Prom Night Massacre*, and opened it in front of her face. Cross-eyed, she flipped through the pages to her place.

* * *

Her father. What a loser, thought Tanya. A *sculptor!* Not that he ever managed to sell any of his weird creations. She shuddered to recall their pathetic Ford Pinto and the single black-and-white TV they'd been able to afford. Who could blame her mother for dumping him? Or for marrying the knockout, Benz-driving owner of Belvedere Realty? She'd taught Tanya a lot. Get what you want out of life. Get it now. And don't worry about stepping on toes. Or hearts.

Danielle smirked. She'd come across characters like this, in books like this, plenty of times. Ambitious. Unrepentently selfish. Materialistic. Like me, she mused, but with a difference. *They* usually paid for their sins by being stalked, sliced, or sautéed in the end. She lowered the book and looked around with relief. This, thank God, was the real world, where the sharp and unscrupulous got a seat on the bus. Through this world, she knew well, she would waltz unscathed.

She rang for her stop, gathered her things, and ran the gauntlet of stares toward the rear. "Ought to be ashamed," spoke an eggshell-frail dowager. The bus's sudden stop gave Danielle a pretext for lurching in her direction and stepping on her foot before exiting. The woman's agonized howl faded as Danielle innocently crossed the street.

The September sun warmed her shoulders while the breeze off the Pacific played with her sundress.

8

Passing the Cliffside, California, Public Library, she inventoried her image in its windows. Legs: terrific. Bust: classic beach bunny. Hair: blonde, straight, faultless. Face: Pepsi-ad quality. She threw herself a smile. This would be the year she'd hook Drew. She felt sure of it. They were both seniors now, both tall, blond, beautiful, and rich – fabulously rich in his case. He'd had all summer to forget about Charity Chase. He needed someone in the passenger seat of the new BMW his parents had just bought him. Together, they'd be shoe-ins for Prom King and Queen. They'd be the envy of all the Huns – the name proudly worn by those students living in exclusive Hundred Palms Estates. Though the Huns ruled Cliffside High's social life and student government, Danielle dreamed of more: ruling the Huns. The triumphant merger of her looks and Drew's loot would put her on the throne. They'd be Ferdinand and Isabella, minus eighty pounds of flab. She grinned. School was only two weeks old. No hurry, she thought. He'd notice her. She'd make certain of that.

Absently, she turned down Jade Street. She was jerked out of her reverie by the sharp scent of disinfectant, then remembered why her feet had led her there: Community Service. She released a long sigh of martyrdom. An hour a week of unpaid labour, which the school district claimed would provide much-needed aid, increase student sensitivity, and build bridges between youth and community, a programme instituted over the objections of the horrified, Hun-packed student council. Gritting her teeth, Danielle entered Driftwood Manor Convalescent Home, wove her way around obstacles human, inanimate, and indeterminate, and found her way for the second time to the room of Mrs Edwina Witt.

"Surf's up, Winnie. What do you say?"

Propped up in bed, Mrs Witt slowly rotated her white-haired head towards her visitor.

Danielle dropped her pack on the floor and noticed that the room's other bed was empty. "What happened to Mrs What's-her-name?"

Mrs Witt's lips moved diligently, producing minuscule smacks but no words.

Danielle saw that the roommate's table was bare and her family photos missing from the wall. "Well, like they say, death happens. Especially to you Model Ts in here." Collapsing into a chair, she prised off her sandals with her toes and extended her feet onto Mrs Witt's bed. "Hope you don't mind. Long day today. I'm totally beat."

Mrs Witt's lips wriggled.

"Well, that's two of us," Danielle spoke for her. She tilted her head up towards the wall-mounted television and gazed blankly at Mrs Witt's news programme. Bending forwards with a groan, she snatched the remote control from the bed, flicked ahead thirteen channels – Mrs Witt's eyes expanding with each change – and found the music video station. Bleeding Ulcer, her favourite group, was on. She leaned back, tossed the remote on the bed, then spotted Mrs Witt's hand crawling toward it.

"Now, now." Danielle nudged it out of reach with her foot, then wondered if the raucous music might draw a nurse to the room. Groaning again, she got to her feet, closed the door to the hall, then locked it. Returning, she spied on a shelf the box of chocolates she recalled from the week before and brought it with her to her chair.

"It's only polite to offer your guests something to eat," she said. Mrs Witt's lips moved speechlessly while Danielle fished among the chocolates. She'd already eaten all the cherry truffles during her first visit. She now plucked out a coconut-covered morsel, examined it critically, took a nibble, grimaced, and spat it out.

"What flavour was that? Turpentine?" She cemented the piece she'd spat out back in place, returned the chocolate to its compartment, then jumped at the sound of two raps on the door.

She shot to her feet and scrambled to find Mrs Witt's programme on the TV. "Just a minute," Danielle crooned. She shoved the chocolates back on the shelf, tugged her sandals onto her feet, straightened her hair, then opened the door. On the other side stood her friend, Brooke.

"Man," hissed Danielle, relaxing. "You scared me." She admitted Brooke and relocked the door. "What are you doing here?"

"My little old lady's on autopilot – asleep, as usual. And *her* TV's broken." Brooke plopped down on the foot of Mrs Witt's bed, grabbed the remote, and flicked forward to the music videos. Bleeding Ulcer's video was over. The two watched ads with scholarly attention, but muted the sound when the next song came on, a pleading ballad by the Rainforest Collective.

"Have you seen the new exchange student?" asked Brooke.

Danielle eyed her friend's stringy red hair and twenty pounds of excess weight. She felt a flicker of pity, then her accustomed pleasure at outshining her. She offered Brooke the box of chocolates, hoping she might gain another pound. "What exchange student?"

"Helga something. From Norway or someplace." She scanned the chocolates. "Any cherry truffles?"

"All gone. They're my favourites, too."

Brooke loudly devoured a peanut cluster. "She's a senior, I think. She's hot," she added, spitting meteors of peanut and chocolate. "Thin and blonde. Cute face. With this little accent when she talks." She licked her fingers. "I passed her in the hall. The guys were practically glued to her. Gavin. Rhett. Jonathan. Drew."

"Drew?" Danielle strained forward at the name.

"Yeah, he was there. Hangin' on her with the rest. Probably praying she'd faint from lack of air so he could give her mouth-to-mouth." Brooke snickered sourly and picked out another peanut cluster. "I hear she lives downtown somewhere. Definitely not in Hundred Palms. Probably no one

12

explained to her that the Hun guys all belong to us."

Danielle's face turned stony.

"Kinda like Charity Chase," added Brooke.

Grimly, Danielle exhaled. "Maybe we'll have to give her the same treatment."

Alarm in her face, Brooke gestured toward Mrs Witt. "Don't worry about her," said Danielle. "She can't talk. Or write either. Look at her hands shake." She glanced at the woman, whose owl-wide eyes stared fixedly back at her. "And what have we got to hide anyway? Charity fell off the cliff."

"After we chased her. Straight towards the edge."

"*We* didn't make her trip on that stupid rock."

"But we *did* write a phony suicide note. Or have you forgotten?"

Danielle sighed. "I'm working on it." She looked out of the window. "Does Tiffany know about this Helga?"

"Beats me."

"Better give her a call. Put a watch on Miss Norway. We'll meet here next week and decide if we need to have a talk with her." Danielle stood up. "For her own sake."

CHAPTER TWO

Tiffany simmered with anticipation. Squinting through the video camera's eyepiece, she pressed the PLAY button and beheld what she'd recorded. "It worked!" she crowed to the empty house. In silent awe, she studied the film. Tripod too high, she noted. Not bad-looking. A little bigger than I'd thought. Ought to try it in a skirt.

She pushed the STOP button, adjusted the tripod, then flew to her room and traded jeans for a skirt. Dashing back to her parents' vast bedroom, she composed herself, pressed RECORD, and despite the fact that she had no speaking role, cleared her throat. Look natural, she reminded herself. She took a deep breath, exhaled, then commenced her walk down the length of the room, the camera trained upon her rear end. "Know thyself," her English teacher had commanded the class that day, quoting some ancient Greek writer. Obedient, Tiffany was placing the final piece in the puzzle of her identity and would at last know the unknowable: how her bottom looked to others.

She reached the end of the room. She whirled around, as she'd seen fashion models do, causing her long, brown hair to wrap itself around her face like seaweed. Clawing it away, she smiled seductively at the camera, then pouted, then laughed. She doubled back and repeated her route, this time stopping and bending over, pretending to pick something up off the floor.

She played back the film, grading her posterior for curve, firmness, breadth and bounce. It didn't measure up to Danielle's, but then neither did Tiffany's unremarkable face, flattish chest, and oily skin. Danielle was a natural beauty; Tiffany needed help, which she received in the eleven beauty magazines she subscribed to. She rewound the film and played it again. She was far better-looking than Brooke, she concluded, who was beyond the help of any magazine except *Journal of Plastic Surgery*. Tiffany admired her own lustrous, mahogany hair – her body's greatest attraction. Then she pulled back her head and lowered the tripod slightly. As photographer for the high-school yearbook, she was skilled at handling cameras. Fired with scientific enquiry, she recorded herself in lycra shorts, her underwear, a mini-skirt, her robe, three different bathing suits, then decided to follow her teacher's advice to the end and film herself naked.

She glanced at the clock. It was just 8.05. Her

15

parents had gone to a seven o'clock movie. She had plenty of time. Then again, they sometimes left movies in the middle, if the teenagers sitting around them belched a lot, or talked, or vomited. She checked the curtains, removed the last of her clothes, pressed RECORD, cleared her throat, then jumped at the sound of the phone. It was the one in her room. The call was for her. Throwing on her robe, she shut off the camera, ran down the long hall, and grabbed the receiver.

"Hi, Jonathan," Tiffany purred. "Guess what?" She gave him a moment. "I'm naked."

"Try again," spoke a female voice. "It's Brooke."

Tiffany shut her eyes. "Damn!" She'd been waiting for eons to use that line. She flopped onto her bed. "What do *you* want?"

"Thanks a *lot*."

"I'm sorry, *OK*?"

"And please don't tell me you're back together with Jonathan – again."

"This time it's forever," stated Tiffany. She heard a slurping sound from Brooke's end.

"Just like the other eighty-nine times."

"Eighty-*seven* times. But remember, that's spread out over four years and three months."

"Why don't you two go to the United Nations and have *them* work on it?"

"The war is over?" she stated, ending her declarative sentence with an interrogative rise. "We made up this morning? Before second period?

16

Then we had this quiet, romantic lunch? In the cafeteria? Which was totally empty because there's no pizza on Tuesdays? We decided we're going to get married the day after graduation? We're naming our first child Kent if it's a boy? And Courtney Marie if it's a girl?" Tiffany heard Brooke chewing noisily. "Are you eating or something?"

"Just a bowl of cereal."

Tiffany reached for the latest issue of *Nymphette* and began flipping through it backwards. "The sound is gross, if you're interested."

"Not really," spluttered Brooke.

"Plus, you'll, like, get electrocuted if you drop the receiver into the bowl."

"I'm talking on the speaker phone."

"My luck," Tiffany sighed.

"Thanks a *lot*."

"I'm sorry, *OK*?" Tiffany fell silent, reading an article on oil-free, hydrating, matte make-ups. "So why did you call, besides to pour Niagara Falls into my ear?"

"To let you know that your *fiancé* has been falling all over the new exchange student. If you're *interested*."

Tiffany stiffened. She heard an avalanche of cereal falling into Brooke's bowl.

"She's from Norway," Brooke went on. "Tall, thin —"

"I've seen her," snapped Tiffany. "Hair blonder than blonde. And her skin's so pale you can

17

practically see through it. And her eyes. They're too blue. They give me the creeps. She looked at me in the hall today and I swear I got the chills."

A fresh round of crunching came from Brooke's end. "Danielle said to put a watch on her. She seems to be going after the Hun guys. I saw Jonathan hand her a bar of chocolate today, flashing his number-one smile."

Tiffany tightened her grip on the phone's receiver in place of Jonathan's throat. "The jerk."

"Is that any way to talk about the father of little Courtney Marie?"

"Shut up."

"I'm sorry, *OK*?" mocked Brooke.

Tiffany hung up. She made up her mind to confront Jonathan tomorrow at lunch. Emerging from her dreams of vengeance, she heard voices, listened, then realized that while she'd been talking her parents had returned and quietly climbed the stairs to their bedroom.

She prayed they'd forgotten how to use the video camera.

CHAPTER THREE

"No trouble at all," Jonathan insisted. "It would be a pleasure. Believe me." He guided Helga down the hall, which was nearly empty at lunchtime. "Why should you put up with a locker that doesn't open half the time? And an old, beat-up one at that, way down on the bottom row, where you have to squat down or break your back." He cast a trained eye at her long, slender legs, as if measuring her for a better fit. "Especially when I know of a vacancy." He plucked an index card from his pocket, studied it, then smiled. "In a *much* better neighbourhood." He recognized how much he sounded like his real-estate agent mother. "Close to the bathrooms. And convenient to both the old and new wings."

"You're quite kind to do this for me," said Helga.

Her accent tantalized him as much as the lithe body moving beneath her airy, white dress. He looked at her face, framed by blonde braids, and realized that she wore no make-up. This honesty in body and spirit, so rare among the other girls, drew him as much as her striking looks. She was a tall glass of cold spring water after years of Tiffany and Diet Coke. Gazing at her silver-blue eyes, he felt he'd do anything for her. Making a start, he pulled up at locker 422 and deftly unlocked it.

"I don't know if you had any dessert with your lunch." With a flourish, he opened the door, releasing a bakery's rich fragrance. The plastic shelves he'd installed within held seven slices of chocolate cake.

"Oh, my!" Helga laughed.

Jonathan beamed. This morning, for Community Service, he'd driven the Meals on Wheels van, and had taken the cake from each of the lunches. Pretending puzzlement to his elderly patrons as to why there was no dessert, he'd diverted two pieces into his mouth and the rest to this locker for resale to students. He offered Helga a plate, then one of the plastic forks he'd pocketed in the school cafeteria.

"I ate quite enough at lunch," said Helga.

Jonathan gave her the smile he held in reserve for preferred customers.

"But perhaps just a bit of cake would not hurt," she relented.

His heart rejoiced. Though he was slightly pudgy and shorter than she was, with every bite she'd be reminded that he had other advantages.

They strolled slowly down the hall. Halting at locker 704, Jonathan opened it up to reveal a neatly ordered storehouse filled with pencils, paper, and other items bought at wholesale prices from his father's stationery shop, which he sold more cheaply than the outmatched, bankruptcy-bound student store. Moving on, he paused at locker 932, then thought better of showing Helga his stock of *Playboy*, *Playgirl*, condoms, and other items he'd marked up quite heavily for enduring checkers' questions and pharmacists' stares to acquire them.

They turned a corner and entered the high school's new wing. "Norway..." said Jonathan. He struggled to frame an intelligent question. "I guess you get to do a lot of swimming in the Indian Ocean."

Helga chuckled politely. "Not really. Norway is in northern Europe, next to Sweden."

Jonathan chuckled along with her, making a note to refuse store credit to the lunkheaded jock he'd overheard talking in the showers about Helga, who'd said that Norway was an island off India. "Right. Anyway, I'd like to see it someday."

She finished her cake. "And I have always wanted to see your Yellowstone Park."

He nodded in approval. "In Florida."

Helga's blonde eyebrows curled. "Isn't it situated in Wyoming? In the Rocky Mountains?"

"I *meant* Wyoming." Jonathan was perspiring. "Someday I'll make it there, too, hopefully."

Helga cocked her head. "Do you mean that you hope to visit Yellowstone Park?"

Jonathan looked perplexed. "Yeah."

"Isn't the word 'hopefully' an adverb?"

Jonathan feared to hazard an answer.

"Doesn't it mean 'full of hope'?" she continued, genuinely seeking his help.

Jonathan nodded quickly, hoping to put the topic behind them.

"So what you have said is 'I will visit Yellowstone Park full of hope'." She gave a little laugh. "Or is that perhaps what you meant to say?"

Jonathan searched for safe ground but could find none. "I guess, like, it's an adverb," he said vaguely.

"And please, what does 'like' mean when it's used as you did?"

Jonathan swallowed.

" 'I guess, *like*, it's an adverb'," Helga refreshed his memory.

"It's like…" Jonathan spoke the words with an amnesiac's uncertainty. "It's sort of…" He sighed. "Actually … it doesn't mean anything," he blurted out with sudden comprehension.

Helga's perfect teeth shone in a smile of revelation. "Thank you, Jonathan. I *now* understand."

He exhaled. His harrowing journey through his own country's language and geography had ended. Stopping before locker 1228, he consulted his card and unlocked it.

"Top row. Only five years old. Pristine condition. Unused all last year." Due to declining enrolment, the school boasted numerous unused lockers, their locations and combinations known, it seemed, to no one but Jonathan. With the help of a locksmithing book, he'd learned to change their combinations, which he did with each new tenant in order to protect his monopoly of access. The rent he charged – ten cents a day – to those who wanted two lockers or who wished to trade for a better locale added up when multiplied by the many properties he managed.

"It will be quite nice, I'm certain," said Helga. "Thank you very much, Jonathan."

He gave her a slip with the combination. He'd decided not to charge her and wondered if telling her this would increase her gratitude or bring on a troubling enquiry into his locker empire. "I think you'll be happy here," he said instead. "Mine's just over there."

"How convenient."

The voice wasn't Helga's. Jonathan turned round and found Tiffany planted behind him.

"Hi, Tiff," he stammered.

"Hi, *Turdface*," she shot back.

Jonathan alertly discerned her mood. He prayed that Helga wouldn't ask to have the epithet explained.

"Let's show our foreign guest our excellent manners," he muttered under his breath to Tiffany. Staging an instructive, formal introduction, he pointed a hand at each of the girls.

23

"Tiffany, this is Helga Sandstad. Helga is an exchange student."

Smiling nervously, Helga held out her hand.

Tiffany ignored it. "And *this*," she sneered, "is Jonathan Rice." She backed him into the lockers, bringing her head an inch closer to his with each word. "Jonathan is a lying, despicable, wheeling-dealing, womanizing, swampbreathed, bigmouthed, smallbrained worm! Who I've now broken up with for the eighty-eighth *and last* time and never want to see *again*!" She spat in his face by way of punctuation, spun round, stormed down the hall, then turned and aimed a finger at Helga. "But *you* stay away from him anyway!"

CHAPTER FOUR

Danielle glanced at her tiny gold watch. "An entire *hour* of this?" she moaned. These Tuesday afternoons were worse than orthodontist visits. She gazed at the sleeping Mrs Witt, then grabbed the television's remote control and tried it for the fourteenth time. The screen remained blank. She flung the remote on the bed, striking one of Mrs Witt's lolly-stick legs with a loud clack. The woman shifted in her sleep. Danielle looked disgustedly at the wall opposite the empty bed, where the room's other television perched, likewise broken. Tortured with boredom, she began to read idly through Mrs Witt's mail, but found this cure worse than the cause. With a sigh she opened her pack, pulled out *Hitchhiker from Hell*, and found her place.

She had to flee. Had to run. Fast. She scrambled through the trees and brambles. Whatever it was, it was coming closer. Its thick, gurgling growls shot pinpricks of fear into Stephanie. Lisa was already dead. And Scott. The creature's black beard was matted with *their* blood. Why had she taken the "scenic route" to the cabin instead of the freeway? Why hadn't she checked the gas tank first?

"Because she's a dork," Danielle answered aloud. She closed the book, leaned back in her chair, and found her eyes aimed at Mrs Witt's chocolates. Expecting to find the box empty by now, she reached to pull it off the shelf and was surprised by its weight. She lifted the lid – and exulted to find it was a new box, filled entirely with cherry truffles, her favourites. She popped one into her mouth, closed her eyes, then bit into its cherry heart, savouring the union of chocolate and cherry. In the midst of her ecstasy a knock sounded on the door, followed by a pause, then three more knocks. She licked her fingers. "I'll get there," she said. She placed another chocolate on her tongue, got up with a groan, shuffled to the door, and admitted Brooke and Tiffany.

"You remembered the special knock?" asked Brooke.

"Call me Einstein," answered Danielle. "Saves me the trouble of hiding things, like this box of *cherry truffles*." Her guests' eyes lit. "Not that Brooke wouldn't have sniffed them out in five seconds."

"Thanks a *lot*," said Brooke.

"*Sorry*," Danielle replied, passing the box

26

around. Tiffany sat in a chair. Brooke reclined on the room's empty bed. Wordlessly, the three chewed, sucked, swallowed and licked.

"I love these," Tiffany spoke at last, coming up for air. "Who answered our prayers?"

"Must be a God after all," said Brooke.

"Then how do you explain *both* TVs in this room being broken?" posed Danielle.

Her friends' faces were transformed into grotesque masks of agony.

"*No* TV? Talk about unfair working conditions."

"God's ways are beyond human understanding."

"My little old lady's is broken, too."

"This Community Service is child labour."

"We should be getting overtime for having to smell these old folks."

"And what about hearing their false teeth clicking?"

"Get a load of the wrinkles on this one."

"I think her subscription to *Glamour* ran out."

"Yeah. About sixty years ago."

"Ten Avon ladies with pliers couldn't stretch *that* skin smooth again."

"And what a pair of knockers."

"If you can find 'em."

"If mine ever get like that, shoot me."

"Gladly."

"Thanks a *lot*."

"I'm *sorry*."

27

"Let the meeting come to order!" boomed Danielle. "We're supposed to be talking about Helga, not the living dead around here." She declined the depopulated box of chocolates held out by Brooke. "Anything to report?"

"Gavin was definitely coming on to her?" stated Tiffany. "On Thursday? I saw him waiting outside her last class? Crunching approximately twenty breath mints?"

"Not enough, in his case," said Danielle.

"I saw Jonathan hand her two pens and a ruler from his supply locker," Brooke testified. She polished off the last of the chocolates. "I did *not* see *her* pay him a cent."

Tiffany, playing violently with a strand of her brown hair, strove to show no reaction to this.

"I also saw her," Brooke continued, "riding in Drew's BMW."

Danielle's mouth dropped. "Tell me you're kidding."

Having no boyfriend, Brooke found pleasure in gloating over her attached friends' troubles. "Sorry," she chirped. "It was Friday, after school. It looked like they were headed towards the beach."

Danielle sat stunned. A silence descended, broken only by Mrs Witt's faint breathing.

"So do we all agree that we need to take action?" proposed Danielle.

Tiffany nodded.

"What if the guys are coming on to her instead

of the other way round?" asked Brooke.

"She's encouraging them!" burst out Danielle. It had always seemed easier, and more satisfying, to discipline a rival female than a straying male Hun. "They're Huns and they belong to us. If she doesn't understand that, we have to make her understand."

"Has anyone *told* her the rules?" Brooke asked.

"I did, on Friday," snapped Tiffany. "All she said was something about how *interesting* the customs here were. And that afternoon, she goes driving with Drew."

Danielle clenched her teeth. "She's been warned. Now it's time to do something. Actions speak louder than words, like they say."

"Just ask Charity Chase," said Brooke.

"I'm not saying we use nuclear weapons. Just show her we're serious. Any ideas?"

A second silence descended. Brooke burped.

"Break into her gym locker and rub poison oak on her clothes?" offered Tiffany.

Danielle smiled briefly. "Whoever did it would probably get poison oak, too."

The air was heavy with cogitation.

"Tiffany's good with cameras," said Brooke. "She could film her in the showers or something and threaten to show it to all the guys."

The words disquieted Tiffany, bringing to mind her recent escapade with the video camera. She'd been lucky to snatch the tape the next morning, and for safety had recorded over it with Billy

Graham's Las Vegas crusade.

"Good thinking," mocked Danielle. "We show it to the guys and then the *entire male student body* goes crazy over her."

"I'm just *trying* to help," Brooke pouted. Tiffany suddenly stood. "You just did."

The two others turned to face her. "What have you got?" asked Danielle.

"An idea that'll get the job done, I think." Tiffany smiled mysteriously. "All I'll need is her photograph."

CHAPTER FIVE

Drew finished the test and glanced discreetly at Helga, one desk away. She was still on the essay, her hand producing her distinctive, filigreed penmanship. He found it, and its maker, bewitching. She flipped her page over and continued writing, leading Drew to wonder whether he'd written enough himself. He was the only Hun male in this honours history class; Hun womanhood was wholly unrepresented. He recalled with a smile the science fair exhibit, devised by some brainy, non-Hun boy, that correlated wealth and blonde hair with low IQ among the female student body. Though blonde, Helga was anything but dumb. Drew identified with her. He too was blond, as well as ridiculously rich, traits beyond his control and which he'd refused to be ruled by.

Though his parents' allowance of $200 a week could have bought him the choicest name-brand clothes, he proudly wore the same pair of patched, threadbare jeans every day – a streak that had now reached seven months and which had inspired several bets on campus. These savings he diverted to the Sierra Club and other environmental groups that his parents railed against regularly. He was tall and square-jawed, with a quarterback's build but no interest in the job. He preferred reading Thoreau to football diagrams. Similarly, he'd resisted his parents' and peers' nudges down the well-worn path of student council, golf, a career in business, and marriage to a dimwit blonde. He eyed Helga's fascinating handwriting and sensed a different path before him.

The bell rang, ending the day's last class. Drew passed his paper up to the front and hurried to catch Helga. Waiting just outside the door, breath mints clattering round in his mouth like balls on a roulette wheel, Gavin got to her first.

"Wondered if you might want to watch football practice today. A real slice of America." He modestly omitted his role as star halfback. "I could give you a ride home after." He herded the mints into a cheek, then smiled.

"That's extremely kind of you," said Helga. "I'm afraid that today I have too much homework. And, actually, I prefer walking home, in order to get my exercise."

Drew caught her words. "I'm walking today, too." He halted at Helga's other side. "If you don't mind company."

"Not at all," she said.

The racket from Gavin's breath mints grew faint as he retreated down the hall. Drew grinned. He'd played his cards right. He'd recalled that she'd accepted his ride a few days before with some reluctance. She liked exercise. So did he. A good pair of walking shoes probably impressed her more than a BMW. He'd left his in the garage today, and now firmly made up his mind never to drive it to school again. Purchased out of the mountainous profits from his father's exporting firm – selling pesticides outlawed in the US to unsuspecting, impoverished countries – the car had filled Drew with guilt. Walking to school through the fresh-minted morning, he'd felt clean, as if bathed in a Norwegian fjord. Now he and Helga were walking together.

"That's the Hall of Fame," said Drew, serving as her self-appointed guide. They stopped before a case filled with photos. "Cliffside High's most illustrious graduates."

She pointed to a bare spot. "Who used to be there?"

"Franklin Critch. One of Cliffside High's *most* illustrious graduates. Until he was prosecuted for larceny, perjury and mail fraud."

They both laughed and stepped outside. "And that?" Helga indicated a large, bronze plaque set into the ground.

"The student seal," Drew replied. "Which seniors like us can order freshmen to polish, on their knees."

"That sounds rather cruel."

"Exactly. A bizarre encouragement to the strong to find pleasure in dominating the weak." He noticed how well his words flowed in Helga's presence, just as they had with Charity.

"You're a much more interesting guide than the one I was given my first week." Helga smiled at him. "Though, according to Tiffany Boyce, I should not associate with you."

Drew rolled his eyes in disgust. "The old world's rigid class system lives."

They descended a lengthy flight of steps, Drew's mind on Charity Chase. She too had complained about the Hun girls. Drew hadn't taken it too seriously. Her suicide, however, was undeniable, and had tormented him all spring and summer. Only Helga's appearance had caused his foglike grief to begin to lift. For the first time in months, he could see blue sky and feel the sun. He liked the sensation.

They crossed the quad among the other students. Tiffany had no trouble spotting them: Drew in his tie-dyed shirt and patched jeans, paperbacks sprouting from both back pockets, and Helga tall and pale, like a candle borne in a procession. She rose from her bench and headed their way, carrying the Pentax camera she'd checked out from the yearbook office. Although her assignment was to capture student life, recording the full panorama of the campus, the photos she took were conceived, composed and cropped to put only Huns on display. Like the long line of Hun photographers before her, she'd dutifully submit one or two blurry pictures of the Hispanic Student Association's autumn dance, which the Hun editor would squint at and reject.

Today, however, she was not after Huns. She followed Helga and Drew with her eyes. Then she saw Rhett Jones, realized their paths would cross, suddenly remembered she'd broken up with Jonathan, and went through the detailed checklist described in the last issue of *Pulchritude*: back straight, shoulders high, stomach in, breasts out, fingers relaxed, never clenched, mouth nonchalant, teeth almost touching, gait confident but not pushy. She'd been having trouble with the finger and gait elements all day. Getting out of bed, she'd felt strangely stiff, the ache in her joints progressing to the point that she'd hobbled around the track in PE and had toiled to bend back the pop top on her can of Diet Coke at lunch. The pain increased suddenly now, causing her to slow to a stop and miss intersecting with Rhett.

"Damn!" she hissed. She massaged her right hip socket, a manoeuvre not on her checklist. Afraid she'd lose Helga, she pushed on again. The photograph she planned to take would never find its way into the yearbook. *No* picture of Helga would get in, she'd sworn. The photograph would, however, be seen. Tiffany had already made a copy of the flier posted outside the nurse's office. She would very soon make many more and put them up all over school, after substituting Helga's picture for the sketch of the weeping teenage girl, whose face appeared under the bold-lettered confession: "I Didn't Know *I* Was Carrying a Sexually Transmitted Disease." This, she figured, would serve notice both to Helga and the guys swooning over her.

Helga and Drew turned left around the library, leaving her view. Tiffany panicked. She was losing them! She forced herself on, wincing all the while, and was relieved to find they'd stopped by the statue of the cougar, Cliffside High's mascot. Here was her chance – perhaps her last.

"It goes back to primitive man," Drew was saying. "Adopting a totem animal that embodies and protects the tribe."

Tiffany panted wearily towards them, struggling to remove the camera from the case that hung from her neck.

"Straight out of the Stone Age," Drew continued.

Cursing her fingers, Tiffany grimaced, finally got the lens cap off, and crept behind Helga. "Smile!" she said.

Startled, Helga turned. Her pale blue eyes bore into Tiffany's own through the viewfinder. At the same instant, the pain in Tiffany's finger joints flared past endurance. She could no longer grip the camera. She tried to snap the picture, missed the shutter button with her finger, then felt the camera slip from her hands. Mr Yancy, the yearbook advisor, was passing nearby when it smashed into pieces.

CHAPTER SIX

Danielle lay stomach-down on her bed, her eyes shuttling between her geometry book and the television screen. *The Godfather*, her favourite movie, was on. She glanced down and read, for the thirteenth time, the textbook's definition of "bisect". Then she looked up and viewed the scene in which a man woke to find his favourite horse's bloody head in his bed. "Gross," she spoke aloud. But effective, she added privately. The Mafia knew how to make a point. She studied angle DEF in her textbook. She looked up and watched an ad for the Army, in which a gun crew scored a direct hit on an enemy health clinic and then celebrated with high fives. She read the definition of "bisect" again. The movie returned to the screen. She opened her compass, using its pointed tip to clean under her fingernails. She sighed. Two men were talking in the movie. She reread the definition of "bisect". Then the telephone on her night table rang. She shot her hand toward it as if for a life-line.

"Hello."

"It's Tiffany. You busy?"

"Doing homework. But that's OK. I'm ready for a break." Danielle turned over onto her back, watching the movie upside-down. "What's up with Helga? Did your plan come off?"

Tiffany paused. "Not exactly."

Danielle didn't like the tone of her voice. "What happened?" she barked, editing out "nitwit" with great effort.

"Well, she was, like, with Drew?" stated Tiffany. "They were standing by the cougar? And I was about to take her picture? But then my hands sort of *slipped*? And I dropped the camera? On the cement?"

Danielle noisily exhaled her disappointment.

"Mr Yancy was there?" continued Tiffany. "He was practically swearing at me? I thought that I was like dead for sure? Thank God he's such an incredible lecher? I pretended to cry? Then I bent down to pick up the pieces and gave him a good look down my blouse? He stopped yelling? Then he put his hand on my shoulder? He said we could discuss it in his classroom, tomorrow before school?" Tiffany made no mention of her mysterious pains.

"Pack plenty of mace," Danielle advised. She likewise passed over her own malady: in the course of chewing a bagel at breakfast, one of her molars had fallen out, causing a hurried trip to the dentist and much talk of bridges and crowns. She'd been thinking about Helga when it happened. She pictured her now, with Drew, and grasped the compass as if it were a knife.

"So Miss Norway didn't get the point?" Danielle pressed the tip of the compass against her thigh until it hurt.

"Sorry," said Tiffany, her voice guilty.

Danielle returned her eyes to *The Godfather*. A man was running. "Forget it," she snapped. "*I'll* take care of it myself." She hung up the phone. "Nitwit."

Danielle lurked after school the next day until she spied Helga walking home. She followed a block behind her, then turned left on a route of her own. Three hours earlier, at lunch, Danielle had entered the school office, empty save for the parent volunteer who typed and answered the phone. Casually remarking to the woman that she'd heard that her daughter had just received a knife wound, she'd been amazed at how quickly the woman had left and with what ease she'd found Helga's address in the files. She now pulled the paper out of her shorts pocket and pondered the address: 244 Gardenia Court. She'd make sure Helga had time to get there first.

Reaching 1st Street, she came to Frescobaldi's Fish Shop and stepped inside. She cruised the long counter, passing the ordered ranks of crab, sea bass, and red snapper. Then she halted abruptly. Before her lay four salmon. Danielle smiled. Before school, she'd made a rare stop in the library, had found the encyclopedias, and had learned, in the article on Norway, that fish was one of the country's staple foods – especially salmon. The examples before her, cast up on their beach of ice, all lacked heads and tails. This suited her fine. She savoured in memory the scene from *The Godfather* and caught the attention of the man behind the counter.

"One salmon head, please," she said.

A smile shone through the man's walrus moustache. "The head only? I bet you got cats."

Danielle forced herself to smile and nod her head. She hated cats.

The fish seller turned and rummaged through a barrel.

"A big one, if you've got it," she added.

The man's forearm emerged, slick and flecked with scales. He held out a head. Its huge eye and Danielle's regarded each other.

"Do you have one with more blood? Around the throat?"

The man's moustache jerked. "More blood? You kidding?"

"No," she answered matter-of-factly. His look caused her to reconsider. "I mean yes." She tittered in support of the "kidding" explanation. "You're sure it's a salmon?"

"Sure I'm sure."

41

It looked like any other fish head to her. Fortunately, Helga was Norwegian. She'd recognize it the way an American would the Statue of Liberty. The man wrapped it and handed it to her.

"No charge," he said. "For cats." He smiled.

She pitied his poor business sense. "Thanks."

She left the shop and set off down 1st Street, following Clifftop Park across the street, high above the ocean. The day was warm, the sea breeze tousling the park's long row of palm trees. She neared the bench where Charity Chase had been confronted by the Huns on her last night. Staring at it from across the street, Danielle suddenly remembered driving past the park with her parents two days before and seeing none other than Helga sitting there. The coincidence was unsettling. She prised her eyes off the bench and looked elsewhere.

Rose Street, Lily Street, Poppy, Poinsettia...

Danielle felt strangely short of breath. She checked Helga's address once more, then pulled a note from her other pocket. She studied her words: "Stay away from the Hun boys or you're dead meat." On she marched, fuelled by the picture of Helga hearing the doorbell ring, leaving her homework, opening the door, and finding the salmon head on her doorstep, the note clamped in its jaws.

Panting now, Danielle sighted a bus stop ahead and staggered towards it as if it were the promised land. She collapsed on the bench, feeling like one of the relics at the nursing home. She needed energy. She pulled a bar of chocolate from her pack and greedily bit into it, cursing her parents for not letting her drive to school like all the other Huns. If only she hadn't had that fifth accident! And if only the man she'd hit would give her a break and come out of his stupid coma. She pictured herself riding in Drew's BMW, kissing his ear while he changed gear, passing the sorry rows of hand-me-down Fords and Toyotas in the school car park. She took another bite, felt something strange, spat out a chunk of chocolate and caramel, and saw one of her teeth sticking out of it.

"What *is* going on?" she yelled. The old woman who was about to sit beside her chose to stand at a safe distance instead. Danielle plucked out the tooth and was alarmed to see that it wasn't a molar. Her tongue found the vacancy at once, in her upper jaw, just left of centre. She opened her compact and peered in the mirror. She looked like a pirate or a street person. She shuddered and snapped the compact shut. Somehow she'd have to remember to keep her lips closed until the dentist fixed her up.

She climbed to her feet and shuffled down the block, her tongue exploring the new gap with great interest. She tried to recentre her thoughts on her mission and came to Gardenia Court at last. She turned left and trudged a block and a half, puffing as if climbing Mount Everest. The houses were small, well-kept bungalows. She passed numbers 238, 242, 246, then stopped. She pulled out Helga's address and reread it: 244 Gardenia Court.

She plodded to the end of the block, stared disgustedly at the street sign, then at Helga's address once more. "I'm *on* Gardenia Court!" she burst out. She glanced across the street. All the numbers were odd, as she'd known they would be. Lungs wheezing, she backtracked, stopping between number 242, a pink stuccoed house, and its neighbour, number 246. Slowly the thought wormed through her weary brain: Helga's house didn't exist.

CHAPTER SEVEN

Brooke's eyes flickered open. Her dream of being passionately kissed by an unidentified boy melted away like a snowflake. Her mother was shaking her shoulder.

"Time to get up, First Daughter."

The sky was just lightening. Brooke closed her eyes. For three mornings now she hadn't heard her alarm. "Yes, Honoured Mother," she mumbled. Her mother left. With a mighty groan, Brooke raised herself out of bed. She groggily found her way into her robe, reached for the matchbox on her dresser, and sleepwalked through her daily dawn tour, placing sticks of incense in the house's six holders and lighting them. She passed her fifteen-year-old sister, sweeping the house, eyes all but closed. From her brother's room, lined with surfing posters, came his yawned "Yes, Master" and the voice of his tutor instructing him in Chinese verse patterns.

45

She lit the living room's incense stick and pulled her robe over her nose to avoid the scent she'd come to loathe. When, she wondered, would her parents grow out of this idiotic phase? Their family came from Scotland, not China. Had she and her siblings brought it on themselves? It was true that they'd often talked back to their mother, had ordered from catalogues with their father's credit cards, and had refused to perform any household chores. Her parents had bought books on understanding teenagers. They'd tried written contracts and family counselling. Then they'd read the article on parents turning to Confucianism to keep their children in line. "Honoured Father" and "Honoured Mother," obedience to parents, rigid etiquette, cheerful acceptance of one's lot and duties – or a flogging with a bamboo rod. The movement was spreading coast to coast, hailed on TV by ecstatic parents. Brooke lit the last incense stick, vowing that she wouldn't clean up after herself if the smell made her throw up.

She shuffled into the kitchen and made breakfast for her parents and the tutor: omelettes with chives, fresh biscuits, peeled kiwis, and hand-squeezed orange juice. Vaguely, she wondered whether this was the traditional Confucian breakfast. While the adults ate in the formal dining room, she and her siblings hunched in the kitchenette and shared a pot of barley gruel, forbidden to speak but mentally recounting the Golden Age now past.

Brooke returned to her room, washed and dressed, then stepped onto the scale. She'd lost another pound. Gruel and hard labour were good for something at least. Pledging herself to stop sneaking bowls of cereal to her room in the evening, she studied herself in the mirror a moment, then approached more closely. She viewed her left wrist. There was a brown spot of darker skin on it, about the size and shape of a penny, that had been hidden by her robe's long sleeves. She'd never noticed it before.

She sat down at her make-up table and surveyed the skyline of jars and dispensers. She reached for the tube of Jacques Pamplemousse Skin Salve and rubbed some on, without noticeable effect. She followed this with trial applications of pancake make-up, calamine lotion, Warts Away, Ajax cleanser, and lastly, Ponce de Leon 900 Tri-Alpha-Hydroxy Restorative Crême. She remembered it was Friday and rubbed it in harder. Though she hadn't had a date in two years, she fantasized about being asked out tonight, the boy noticing the spot on her wrist, and his spreading the word that she had AIDS, or leprosy. She glanced at the clock. It was nearly 7.30. The dark patch of skin was still visible. Though a heat wave had blown in the day before, she decided to peel off her tank top and put on a white, long-sleeved blouse instead, buttoning the cuffs to hide the spot. She then marched out and drove to school.

She passed Drew, walking on the right, but

didn't stop to offer him a ride. She'd tried that on Thursday and had been turned down. She didn't need more rejection. He'd actually claimed he preferred walking! She snorted. Was she truly that repulsive? The sight of him led her to review her roster of possible dates for that evening. Gavin. Too foul-breathed. Rhett. Too short. They were the only unattached Hun seniors. No wonder Danielle was determined to snare Drew. He was the plum of the Hun senior class, waiting to be picked. Dipping into the junior class, there was Logan. Majoring in substance abuse. Patrick. Too nerdy. Sean. Too much hardware hanging from his ears, a regular walking wind chime. She thought about Ray, the last date she'd had – a nice enough boy who'd been scared off either by her parents' hour-long interrogation or by their Great Dane's endless licking of his testicles. She checked her wrist. The spot was still there. She was mildly alarmed, until she realized there was no one left on her list of dates and that she'd be staying home anyway. Then she remembered Jonathan.

Tiffany had broken up with him. Forever, she'd sworn to Brooke. Having heard the same line on eighty-seven previous occasions, Brooke had ignored it at the time. Now, desperate for a date, she chose to believe it. She parked the car and strode through the gate, her pace quickening. She entered the main building. At once she saw Jonathan, standing like a shopkeeper in front of his stationery supplies locker. She gave her cuffs a tug and approached.

"Hi, Jonathan."

"Hi," he said. With a practised eye he sized her up, saw that she wasn't opening her purse or giving other signs of buying something, and therefore turned his gaze elsewhere.

"How ya doing?" Brooke remembered that her left side was her better one, and slid three steps to the right to offer him that vantage.

"Just fine," Jonathan replied. A girl came up, reached around Brooke, and swung open the locker to look over his wares. "Would you mind moving?" Jonathan addressed Brooke, and motioned her aside. She complied at once, then realized that her bad side was now facing him again. He sold two pencils, bringing each to a perfect point with an electric sharpener as a courtesy.

"So how ya doing?" Brooke enquired.

"You already asked me that."

"What?" She'd been having trouble hearing lately, especially when there was background noise.

"I said, 'You already asked me that'."

Brooke returned three steps to the right. "Oh," she answered. She giggled, hoping to make him feel they'd shared a joke, but his eye was on an approaching customer, whom he moved Brooke aside to accommodate, making a sale of twelve sheets of notebook paper, with a thirteenth thrown in at no charge. The revelation reached Brooke that the way to his heart lay through his wallet. She took out her own and studied his stock.

"I need a pen, actually," she lied. She reminded herself that he might be unattached only very briefly. Some of his break-ups with Tiffany lasted no more than hours. She must seize her chance. "Make that a pack of twelve," she said.

Jonathan's eyebrows arched. He seemed impressed. "At your service," he said, and plucked the package off one of the suction-cupped hooks he'd installed. She knew that she now had his attention, at the cost of $5.49.

"Tiffany says you guys have broken up for good," Brooke remarked, inspecting his box of special markdowns.

"You got it."

"Must be kind of lonely. You know. In the evenings." She dared not look at him when she said it.

"Not really," Jonathan answered.

He exchanged greetings with two passersby. Brooke feared she was losing his attention. She put a box of paper clips in his hand.

"I've been reading a lot," he volunteered.

She read now and then. She wondered if she should propose that they read together tonight. It sounded weird. Then she remembered that he sold *Playboy* at another locker. Should she buy one and then suggest that they read the hilarious advice letters? This would get him pointed in the right

50

direction, as well as adding $6.95 to his till. She debated furiously with herself.

"Whatcha been reading?" she asked, stalling for time in which to make her decision.

"Plays, mainly."

"No kidding. Sounds heavy." She noticed that he was an inch taller than she was – the ideal height difference, according to *Glamour*. Had he been the one kissing her in her dream. "Yeah," he said. "Pretty heavy all right. I'm on *The Wild Duck* right now."

"What?" Pretending to brush back her red hair, Brooke stealthily cleaned her left ear with a finger, hoping this might improve her hearing.

"*The Wild Duck*," he repeated loudly. "By Ibsen."

She added a pair of erasers to her account, knowing full well she owned dozens already. "Who's he?"

"A playwright," he said. "From Norway."

Brooke felt her face fall.

"I've got his collected works. He's probably the most famous writer from there."

Brooke's plans fled her mind. Her hopes collapsed. Rage crackled into flame inside her.

"And what brought this on?" Her voice was unsteady. She strained to seem ignorant of the answer, praying that perhaps she was wrong.

"You know Helga? She turned me on to him," Jonathan casually replied. She saw that his eyes brightened at the name. "I heard her mention him in class. Thought he might be worth checking out."

Brooke's fury blazed. Though she'd joined the war against Helga half-heartedly and only so as not to be left out, she now boiled with visions of vengeance and yearned to utterly destroy her.

"She said she'd help me with this latest one after school today," Jonathan added. Pleasant expectation flickered on his face.

Brooke's patience snapped. Tears gathered in her eyes. He was just like all the rest – a slave to anything thin and blonde.

"And after your stupid plays," wailed Brooke, "you read the letters in *Playboy* out loud I bet!" She knew she was shouting but didn't care.

Jonathan stood before her, dumbstruck.

"Then you'll look at the pictures, *of course!*"

He cocked his head in puzzlement. "What?"

"You can keep your pens and erasers!" screamed Brooke. She snatched the box of paper clips she'd meant to buy, raised it high, and opened it, letting them rain out onto the floor. She presented him with a vengeful smile. Then she looked up and saw that the deed had caused her sleeve to slip down towards her elbow. On the back of her hand, in plain view to all, were three new dark spots, one of which was shaped exactly like a skull. Brooke let out a shriek and fled.

CHAPTER EIGHT

"Turn left!" Tiffany ordered.

"What did you say?" asked Brooke.

"*Left!*"

Brooke swerved into the left lane and turned sharply, following the red Corvette and throwing Danielle against the door. It was Sunday morning. They were on the way to the beach, but had decided to first follow cars driven by handsome males. "Born to Hate" by Wehrmacht was blaring from the radio, the SERVICE ENGINE SOON light flashing on and off in time with the beat.

"Tinted windows!" shouted Danielle above the music. "He must be rich."

Brooke sped to keep up with the car. "Or maybe just albino." She'd been trailing it for miles when suddenly the driver pulled over and parked. Brooke slammed on her brakes and parked behind him, staring like the other girls. The Corvette's door swung open. From inside came a short, vastbuttocked, cigarillo-smoking woman, who extricated herself in stages and was followed, like a mother bear leaving her den, by her waddling, diaper-wearing cub.

There was stunned silence in Brooke's car, apart from "Full Dumpster of Love for Ya" by Trash on the radio.

"Damn," summed up Tiffany.

"Beauty's only skin deep," said Danielle.

"I think you mean 'You can't judge a book by its cover'," Brooke spoke up.

"Just shut up and drive," snapped Tiffany.

"*You're welcome!*" Brooke shouted.

"*Sorry!*" mocked Tiffany.

The episode was in character with the previous week's events. Nothing had been going right in the effort to separate Helga from the Hun boys. The beach outing was less a tanning session than an emergency meeting of the Joint Chiefs of Staff, who were determined now to destroy their enemy.

Brooke backtracked nearly five miles, headed up the coast highway, and turned off into the Sycamore Club, which all three girls' parents belonged to. They got out and made their way down the boardwalk. Danielle subtly kept their pace slow, so as not to start wheezing from shortness of breath in front of the whole beach crowd. This suited Tiffany, who wished to hide the gimpy gait caused by her ever more painful hip joints. Though it was nearly ninety, Brooke was wearing a shirt of her father's over her swimsuit. It was long enough to reach her fingertips, and both cuffs were buttoned tightly to hide the half dozen spots she sported on each hand. She prayed that no one would ask her the reason.

They stepped onto the sand and chose a site with a view of the volleyball court. In silence, they slathered on their sunblock, reluctant to tackle the matter at hand. Danielle put on her Walkman's headphones and listened to *Serenity Cove*, a tape of beach sounds that her parents, hard-driving stockbrokers, played to wind themselves down in the evenings. Tiffany flipped backwards through an issue of *Psst!*, pausing at an article on tinted moisturisers. Brooke discreetly opened her compact and arranged her red hair over the small dark spot she'd found on her forehead that morning.

"Shall we get it over with?" Danielle suggested an hour later.

Tiffany had at last reached her magazine's table of contents. She raised her head. "So what happened with *your* plan?"

Danielle's face soured at the memory. "I was going to leave this fish head on her doorstep. I found her address, but when I got there, there was no stupid house with that number." She omitted the added insult that liquid from the fish had leaked into her pack.

"No house?" mused Tiffany. "Pretty weird."

"Leaving a fish head is even weirder," said Brooke. "No wonder your backpack smells like a bait shop."

Danielle sniffed it. She wondered if the smell explained Drew's retreat when she'd tried to entice him into walking home with her on Friday. Or had her temporary false tooth, installed by her dentist, been askew? She felt it with her tongue. It was simply wedged in place between its neighbours and tended to swing out like a dog door if she bit into anything hard.

"You got any better ideas?" she challenged.

Tiffany propped herself up on her elbows. "Why not ask the other Hun girls to help out?"

"Nicole Cappellini said she'd help," replied Danielle. "If she's not too busy with student council, cheerleading, French Club, Nostalgia Club, and the Other groups she belongs to. The others all said they weren't interested."

The three ruminated in silence. Tiffany got up to go to the toilet, walking slowly both to spare her joints and to advertise her existence to all boys within view. Her luscious brown hair swung alluringly back and forth, halfway down her back.

"I was driving by the park?" Tiffany remarked when she returned. "On Thursday? Going home from Community Service? I, like, looked over? And there was Helga? Sitting on the bench?"

The others knew what bench she meant. In unison, all three girls looked down the coast to where the beach disappeared. The waves there threw themselves into the massive rocks below Clifftop Park, the same rocks onto which Charity Chase had fallen to her death.

"Why does she have to pick *that* one?" asked Danielle.

No one offered a reply.

"She was here at the beach yesterday," said Brooke. "By the lifeguard station. She was reading. Plays." She thought acidly of Jonathan. "She said 'Hi' when I passed. She'd been there all day. What's strange is that she never gets sunburned, even with her fair skin." Brooke stated this last fact with disgust. She, by contrast, turned red and peeled if she stood in front of a forty-watt bulb. She seethed at Helga's good luck in this and every other category.

Four boys started playing volleyball, freezing the girls' conversation. One was a Cliffside graduate, famed for his many drink-driving arrests, whose talents had been foretold when he'd been found drunk behind the wheel of his car simulator in Driver's Education. He was well-built and looked over at Tiffany. Following the advice of an article in *Psst!*, she pretended not to notice him and quickly reopened the magazine, feigning reading an article on codpieces, plague, pilgrimages and other fads that, after a long sleep, were fashionable again.

"C'mon!" barked Danielle. "We're here to think. Get your nose out of your magazine."

"As soon as you take off your headphones," said Tiffany.

"You sound like my parents!" snarled Danielle. She ripped off the headphones and snapped off her Walkman.

"Now who has an idea for taking care of Helga *for good?*" she demanded. She was annoyed by Tiffany's lack of focus as well as by the fact that the boy had chosen to cast his gaze at Tiffany rather than at her.

"What did you say?" Brooke enquired.

"Christ Almighty! Are you deaf or something? And what are you doing with your shirt on? It's boiling!"

Brooke ransacked her brain for an excuse. "I get freckles!" she blurted out truthfully. "Even with sunscreen. I'm not like Helga."

"I'll say," said Tiffany.

"Thanks a *lot!*"

"I'm *sorry.*" Tiffany became aware of her urgent need to pee again, a need she'd felt much more often lately. Too embarrassed to make yet another trip to the toilet, afraid of what Danielle might say, she hooked her ankles and pressed her legs together. Just then an ice-cream seller approached. Grabbing her wallet, Tiffany found her finger joints so swollen and painful that she couldn't manage to open the clasp. Enviously, she watched as Brooke bought an ice-cream sandwich. Danielle eyed Brooke hungrily as well, dying to buy one, too, but afraid that her false tooth might come out and get lost in the sand.

"So who the hell's got an idea?" cried Danielle.

The others avoided her angry eyes. Brooke aimed hers at the two girls who'd joined the volleyball game. Both seemed cut from Tiffany's magazine: tall, slender, perfectly tanned. One was a brunette who seemed to enjoy maintaining suspense in her audience as to when, in the course of her leaping and diving, her bikini's top would lose its load. The other had long, dazzling blonde hair, straight as a waterfall running down her back. Brooke stared at it, hating it and everything it stood for. It was nearly as long and as light as Helga's. Suddenly she had an idea.

"Why don't we cut off her hair?" she proposed.

CHAPTER NINE

When Monday's last bell rang, Nicole Cappellini was the first one out of her business class. She was in a merry mood as she hurried down the hall, having just racked up a profit of $10,000 in the classroom's mock stock market. By the time she reached Helga's classroom, she'd mentally spent the bulk of it. She positioned herself outside the door, just as Danielle had instructed her. The class was a few minutes late getting out. She spent some more of her profits, acquiring a French chateau and a new hair dryer.

Abruptly, the door swung open and the first students began pouring out. Nicole noticed a clattering sound. She turned and discovered Gavin beside her, breath mints loudly orbiting his mouth. She knew he often waited for Helga. She wondered if he'd throw off the plan.

"Mint?" he offered. His breath held the natural foulness and chemical freshness found in veterinarians' waiting rooms.

Nicole shook her head, then spotted Helga approaching the door, talking to Drew. What if he walked home with her? Nicole's pulse quickened at the thought.

"That's just what Thoreau was saying," said Drew. He and Helga emerged from the room. "Cut your *expenses* so you won't have to waste your life working to pay your bills!"

Nicole was shocked by such heresy. No wonder Thoreau had been hanged with the witches. Or was that Benedict Arnold? She approached Helga and put in place the same oversized, phony smile that her mother often wore. She opened her mouth to speak, at which moment Gavin stepped forward, eclipsing her.

"Wondered if you might want to see a movie with me this afternoon," he asked Helga. "*Grievous Bodily Harm Eleven* is playing at the Cliffside Twelve-Screen."

He sent the mints on a quick circuit. "A real taste of America."

Helga walked down the crowded hall, surrounded as if by a ring of reporters.

"By not *having* to work, Thoreau could study nature and write," Drew went on.

Nicole grimaced, wondering how someone as rich and handsome as Drew could have gone so far astray.

"Thank you," said Helga to Gavin. "It sounds quite interesting. But today I must study."

61

"It's nothing at all like *Grievous Bodily Harm Ten*," Gavin persisted. "Maybe that came to Osaka."

"Oslo," Helga politely corrected.

Nicole trailed along, perspiring, aware that the scene was beyond her control. Fortunately, the procession was following the route that Danielle had predicted. As they all headed outside towards the gym, there was a half second of silence in the conversation. Nicole pounced.

"As a member of the Cliffside High World Friendship Club..." she spoke up.

"A total farce," Drew informed Helga, as if he were translating. He knew that the club was no more than a group of Hun bigwigs on the student council, who voted themselves a budget each year and spent it dining at restaurants specializing in foreign cuisines.

"*Grievous Bodily Harm Ten* stank, I'll admit," Gavin butted in. "A waste of money. Unless you were doing your PhD on blood circulation."

Drew pulled Thoreau's *Journal* from his back pocket. "'That man is richest whose pleasures are cheapest'," he quoted.

Helga smiled in response.

In panic, Nicole realized that they were getting close to the cloakroom. Why had she offered to help Danielle? She cleared her throat and reinstated her Miss America smile.

"On behalf of the club, I would like to invite you to address our group at —"

A mint escaped from Gavin's mouth and struck her neck, sliding under her dress. Nicole gave a small shriek.

"Sorry," said Gavin. He reached towards her playfully. "I'll get it."

"Get away from me!" she yelled. Her smile and patience took flight. "All of you!"

The three others froze.

"Except for you, Helga." She stared at her. "We have something to discuss."

Gavin drifted off. Drew told Helga goodbye. Nicole regained her composure, amazed that losing it had accomplished her end: escorting Helga alone.

"The club," she continued, "asked me to invite you to give a talk to us on Nepal."

"Norway?" asked Helga.

"Norway. Of course." Nicole commenced a series of wriggles, followed shortly by the sound of Gavin's mint hitting the ground.

"That would be a great pleasure," said Helga.

Nicole smiled. She viewed Helga's hair, unbraided today and incomparably sexy. Cutting it off would truly be just this side of murder. She congratulated Brooke on her plan.

"We wrote out a formal invitation." Nicole pawed through her purse, then looked up. "I know it's here. I was going to check my make-up in the cloakroom, right there. Come in for a second and I'll find it for you."

Nicole led the way. There was no one around.

She opened the door, followed in by Helga.

At once Brooke and Danielle rushed from the cubicles, wearing tracksuits and ski masks. They grabbed Helga's arms. Nicole gave a soft, unconvincing scream and fled. Tiffany then burst out of the last cubicle. Through her mask's eye holes she found Helga's hair, grabbed a thick strand with one hand, then held up a pair of scissors with the other as if she were a sacrificial priestess. Helga struggled mightily, but was unable to free herself. Then she looked into Tiffany's eyes. Suddenly the pain in Tiffany's fingers, severe already, soared past bearing.

"Do it!" growled Danielle.

Tiffany's hands felt paralyzed. Behind her mask she grimaced in torment. The scissors slipped from her fingers and fell. Slowly she crumpled to her knees.

Helga next faced Brooke, who found herself instantly flooded with fatigue. Astounded, she felt the strength in her muscles draining away uncontrollably. Her grip on Helga's arm loosened. Then her entire body went limp. She sank to the floor beside Tiffany.

Danielle was aghast at these defections. When Helga peered at her, she was already panting desperately for breath. Her lungs now began to wheeze as loudly as a pump organ's bellows. Forgetting the plan, intent on survival, she released Helga's other arm and slid onto all fours.

Panting herself, free now, Helga regarded her

prostrate assailants. Their breathing was heavy. They seemed as helpless as infants. She reached down, grasped the top of Tiffany's mask, and tugged it off. She did the same with Brooke's. Then Danielle's. None dared look up at her.

Helga's voice was wobbly but determined. "There will be justice," she declared. "I promise. That's why I've come." She kicked the scissors across the room. Then she disappeared out of the door.

It was ten minutes before Tiffany could speak.

"We'll get suspended for this for sure."

All three were still sitting in a stupor on the floor.

"All of a sudden I was totally weak," said Brooke. "It's like she has magical powers."

"Superhuman," Tiffany agreed.

Danielle inhaled, her chest expanding. "You're right. She does." She breathed out slowly. "And getting suspended is the least of our problems."

The others faced her. Danielle, eyes closed, filled her lungs again.

"Helga isn't mortal," she stated. "She's a ghost. The ghost of Charity Chase."

CHAPTER TEN

"A ghost," moaned Tiffany.

"Get serious."

"I am," said Danielle. The others gawked at her.

"Why don't we talk somewhere else," Brooke suggested.

The three climbed slowly to their feet. Tiffany peeked out of the cloakroom door. "No sign of Helga. Or the principal."

They stuffed their tracksuits and masks in their backpacks and shuffled towards the car park.

"A *ghost*?" brayed Brooke. "You've got to be kidding."

They reached Brooke's tan Toyota and stopped.

"I wish I were," Danielle replied.

Brooke cocked her head. "You mean you go to *Norway* when you die?"

Danielle rolled her eyes. "Don't you guys ever read?"

"Like what?" asked Tiffany.

"Like *Death Of a Nerd*, *A Demon Among Us*, *Bridge Over the River Styx*. The ghosts of the murdered are always coming back to earth."

"In *books!*" yelled Tiffany.

"And in real life, too! I've already seen two ghosts in my life before now. And let me tell you, they weren't made up." Danielle shivered at the thought. "If *you* haven't seen one, you just haven't been in the right place at the right time. But you sure as hell are now."

The other two eyed her uncertainly.

"It's a classic case. I should have caught on sooner." Danielle kicked a rock. "All the signs were right there."

"Like what?" asked Brooke.

"Like open your eyes! The first day of the first school year *without* Charity Chase, a new girl shows up, out of the blue. From a faraway country, at the ends of the earth."

Brooke and Tiffany pondered these facts with sudden trepidation.

"When I went to her house, it *didn't* exist. Naturally! She's a spirit!"

Shaken, Brooke leaned on the car for support. "And her favourite place to sit?" pressed Danielle.

"On the bench in Clifftop Park," Brooke and Tiffany answered in unison.

"Talk about totally obvious," Danielle scolded herself. "They *always* come back to the place where they died."

Tiffany swallowed. "If she's a ghost, how come

67

you can't stick your hand right through her?"

"They get bodies when they come back to earth," said Danielle. "But not like ours. They're just shells. Just look at her. Her hair's beyond blonde. And her skin's too pale and bloodless for a mortal's."

"And it never sunburned," remembered Brooke.

Tiffany stiffened. "My God," she muttered. "That's why she left biology class the day we all pricked our fingers to draw blood."

Brooke screamed. "I can't believe this is happening!"

"Why is she back?" Tiffany demanded.

"For the same reason ghosts *always* come back to earth," said Danielle. "To avenge her death!"

"You're sure she knows we did it?" asked Brooke.

"Of course she does!" Danielle shot back. "You heard her yourself: 'There will be justice'."

"'That's why I've come'," Tiffany repeated, suddenly understanding the words.

"You bet it's why," declared Danielle. "She really gave herself away with that line."

Brooke's eyes were wild. "What's she going to do to us?"

"She's already started," said Danielle.

The other two girls locked their eyes on hers, waiting to learn their fates.

"I didn't want to tell anybody. But I've been having trouble breathing lately." Danielle looked away from the others. "It's been getting worse for a week now. It's like I'm turning into a little old lady." She considered removing her six false teeth, but decided that her point was clear.

"That's weird," said Brooke. She unbuttoned her right shirt cuff and pulled it back. Her audience grimaced. A dozen dark spots were spread out like islands over the back of her hand. One unmistakably resembled a skull.

"Jesus," whispered Danielle. "Liver spots."

"What?" asked Brooke.

"*Liver spots!* Old people get 'em. My grandmother's even got 'em on ..."

Brooke pulled back her hair, revealing four more high on her forehead.

"On her head," Danielle finished. She examined the skull-shaped spot and smirked. "Nice of her to make sure you got the message."

"And I think," added Brooke, "that my hearing's starting to go. A little."

"A lot," said Tiffany. She noticed the other two looking at her.

"Well?" asked Danielle.

Tiffany was silent. Then tears began to overflow her eyes. "When I blew it that time? Taking Helga's picture? It was all because of *this*!" She held out her hands for public inspection. Her knuckles were swollen, her fingers bent like claws. "Sometimes the pain's so bad I want to scream."

"Sounds like arthritis," Danielle diagnosed.

"What's *happening* to us?" wailed Tiffany.

"Helga," Danielle replied. "You said it yourself.

She has magical powers. She could have killed us back in the cloakroom. Or any other time she wanted. But instead, she picked out a punishment for us that's *worse* than death – getting old!"

The three peered at each other, their faces frozen by this revelation.

Brooke's eyes lost their focus, then seemed to turn inward, beholding the dawn of mortality. "Are we going to die? Soon, I mean?"

"Beats me," Danielle replied.

Simultaneously, Brooke and Tiffany exploded into tears.

"I *knew* we never should have met Charity at night!" blubbered Tiffany.

"Especially at the edge of a cliff!" added Brooke.

It had all been Danielle's plan. She avoided their eyes.

"I'm too young to die!" Tiffany informed the universe at the top of her lungs.

"You're getting older by the minute," mused Danielle.

Tiffany faced her accusingly. "*You* got us into this! Now get us out! Or my ghost will kill you deader than dead. If Helga doesn't get you first."

"You think I don't want to?" Danielle shouted back. "Unfortunately, it isn't that easy. You can't kill a ghost. I'm sure of that, from what I've read in books. But let me look back through some of them. Once in a while the spirits get beaten. At least we can maybe get some ideas."

"Hurry!" said Brooke. She opened the door of her car and urged Danielle inside. "I'm having my birthday party in two weeks!"

CHAPTER ELEVEN

Tiffany flicked her windshield wipers to MEDIUM. It was Tuesday night. Though normally she hated rain, in this case it suited her perfectly. It meant fewer people on the streets and fewer witnesses to her errand.

She followed Fourth Street out of Cliffside and into neighbouring Wilmington Heights. Children's boutiques and outdoor cafés gave way to bars and self-storage lockers. She recalled where she was and locked the car doors. She turned onto Broadway, swerving around a drunk talking to himself in the street. The rain was now drumming deafeningly on the roof of the car. "Shut up!" she yelled back. She turned the wipers to HIGH and struggled to make out the numbers on the buildings. "Where the hell is 930?" she demanded. She drove five more blocks, glimpsed 924, crept past a pawn brokers', and parked. She sighed. She would be safe here, from prying eyes if not from rape. She got out and limped toward the drugstore. When your mission was buying adult nappies – for yourself – confidentiality won out over price, selection and personal safety.

She stepped inside. The store seemed empty. A hefty, grim-visaged female clerk, guarding the register like a dragon, took note of her entrance without greeting. Tiffany disappeared down an aisle. Another customer entered the store. Tiffany ducked down instinctively. She wondered if she really needed the nappies, then thought back with a shudder to her close calls in English and history, and suddenly sensed her bladder's fullness. She scanned three aisles, then found what she was seeking at last and gave silent thanks. She debated between Second Childhood and Sphincter Sentry, picked up three packages of the former, then made her way to the front.

"I'm buying these for my great-grandmother?" she announced, unbidden, to the clerk. "She just came to live with us? From Kansas? It's the very brand she asked me to get? The same brand she used to use? Back in Kansas?"

The clerk stared at her. "Where in Kansas?"

Tiffany swallowed. "Dallas," she answered out of the blue, praying it was located in that state. The woman eyed her. Waiting for judgement, Tiffany suddenly realized that she was beginning to pee.

"Nice town," said the clerk, approving her answer. "I've been there two or three times."

Tiffany had trouble maintaining eye contact. A

Nirvana-like bliss passed over her face, followed by deep worry.

"That'll be nineteen dollars and sixty-eight cents," said the clerk.

Tiffany paid, requested a brown bag, and furtively eyed her small puddle. Her jeans and left shoe held most of the urine. She took a trial step, getting used to the feel, then remembered the storm with relief.

"Floor's a little wet," she remarked offhandedly. "From the rain."

The clerk bent over the counter to look.

Tiffany peered in panic at her bright yellow urine. "They say this storm has a lot of acid rain in it," she added and vanished out the door.

Tiffany awoke the next morning wondering how she would get out of bed. Each joint in her body felt swollen twice its size. She glanced out of the window. It was still drizzling. Vaguely, she recollected a commercial in which an old lady complained of wet weather worsening her arthritis. She winced as she slowly sat up in bed, vowed to move immediately to the Sahara, then staggered gingerly to the bathroom. She picked up a bottle of aspirin and squinted, hoping to see the word "arthritis". For the past two days she'd found it increasingly hard to focus on nearby objects. She gave up reading the minuscule type, took two pills anyway, then stood under a scalding shower. Combing her hair afterwards, she noticed the comb felt heavy in

74

her hand. She glanced at it. Then, in a frenzy, she wiped the condensation from the mirror. Ragged gaps showed in what had been her body's prize attraction: her gorgeous brown hair was falling out.

"Damn that Helga!" she swore aloud. She blinked back tears while surveying the damage. She would have no choice but to wear her hair up. Then she set eyes on her ravaged fringe. She couldn't let that show either. After dressing and pinning up her hair, heaping curses on Helga all the while, she covered her scalp with a red bandana, as she'd seen her mother attired in photos taken back in the sixties. She hoped her peers would find the look cool. Then she searched her magazines for advice, flipped to page twenty in April's *Foxy*, and skimmed in disappointment the article titled "Your Balding Boyfriend: What To Do, What Not To (and Ten Remarks To Keep *Under* Your Hat!)." She looked at her clock. She had to be at school early. She dragged her body to the kitchen, washed down a croissant with a Diet Coke, trudged out to her car, lurched back to the house, distastefully put her nappy in place, then shuffled back out and drove to school.

Brooke pulled into the space right behind her. The rain had stopped. They parked and got out.

"What's that?" asked Brooke, pointing at Tiffany's bandana.

"A bandana, idiot. What do you think?"

"*Sorry*," said Brooke. "I was just wondering

75

why you came to school disguised as a Russian cabbage farmer."

This was not precisely the response that Tiffany had hoped for. She lowered her voice to a deathbed whisper. "My hair is falling out."

Brooke's eyes expanded. The pair set off, Brooke slowing her steps to match Tiffany's hobble. She scoured her brain for a change of topic. "So why are you here so early today?"

"Mr Yancy," answered Tiffany. "I have to help the old lecher twice a week to pay off the camera I broke. Today he'll be taking more pictures of me."

"With or without clothes?"

"*With*. Are you crazy?" Then she imagined him arranging her pose, carefully adjusting her buttocks with his hands – something that seemed to need doing often – and causing her nappy to audibly crinkle. She tried to evict the vision from her mind. "What are you doing here, anyway?"

"I thought I'd work out in the gym before school."

Tiffany scented deception. "Yeah?"

"Maybe do some gymnastics."

The word sent more pain into Tiffany's joints. "When did this start?"

Brooke didn't answer. Then Tiffany realized she was crying.

"This morning," she sniffled.

Tiffany halted, alarmed. "Helga?"

Brooke nodded her head. "My clothes haven't been fitting lately. The way they used to." She dabbed at her eyes. "This morning I measured myself. And I'm *shrinking*!" She gave herself up to unrestrained bawling.

Tiffany viewed her in terror. It was true. Brooke was shorter by an inch or two. "Jesus Christ," she murmured.

"I thought maybe hanging from the bars might help," Brooke wailed miserably.

Tiffany patted her shoulder. "Of course it will." Privately, she had her doubts.

Brooke mopped up her tears. They inched down a walkway, Tiffany fantasizing about being pushed in a wheelchair. Then both of them halted. In the distance, Helga crossed between two buildings.

An eerie chill skittered up Brooke's spine. Both girls exhaled when she disappeared.

"How am I supposed to pass her in the hall?" said Brooke. "Knowing what we know?"

"Not to mention what *she* knows," said Tiffany.

They pushed on in silence.

"At least we haven't been called in to the dean's office for trying to cut her hair," Brooke spoke up. "It probably would have happened by now."

Tiffany sighed. "Great. So now we know for sure that she couldn't care less about that. She's after revenge for Charity."

Brooke cleaned out her left ear. "For what?"

"For *Charity*," Tiffany repeated.

"Clarity?"

"Charity!"

Brooke nodded. "I almost wish she'd get it over with. And put us out of our misery."

Tiffany grabbed her arm for help in ascending a short flight of steps. She rested at the top, then put her mouth to Brooke's ear and shouted, "Me, too."

CHAPTER TWELVE

1.30. 1.48. 2.17. 2.27. *Time flies when you're having fun*, Danielle mocked herself. It was Wednesday night and insomnia, not fun, was what she was having. It was the latest symptom of her advancing age. She hadn't minded the first two nights, when she'd been madly skimming her horror novels in search of help against Helga. Now, however, the bags under her eyes were as big as gunnysacks. She hungered for sleep. She'd tried warm milk. She'd counted sheep, Gucci purses, new BMWs. She now tried guided fantasy, strolling hand in hand with Drew along the beaches of Bermuda, listening to him marvel aloud at her physical and spiritual beauty. When this failed, she turned to truly desperate measures: her history textbook.

She opened Chapter Five of *Let Freedom Ring* and forced herself to read. Looking ahead, she held great hopes for the discussion of the Stamp Act crisis, and was astounded to discover herself still awake at the end of the chapter. Though Chapter Six, "The Tide of Independence", promised to induce sleep, and possibly death, she couldn't bring herself to administer the dose. Instead, she scanned her paperbacks for any she'd missed, reached for *A Score to Settle*, and opened a page at random.

Rolf's lips met hers. Ashleigh closed her eyes and fell deeply into the kiss. Down and down, plunging blindly into the unknown, the voices in her head growing ever fainter. Her father yelling that he wished she'd died in the car wreck instead of her beautiful sister, that she was ugly, that no boy would ever kiss her. Margo saying that Rolf gave her the creeps. Megan saying he had the eyes of a killer. Old Mrs Weiss remembering that a man by the same name had been executed fifty years ago – for murder.

The plot came back to her. She closed the book. It wouldn't help with Helga. Though Rolf was a ghost, no one was able to stop him from killing the descendants of the jurors who'd falsely convicted him. Would she soon be as dead as his victims? Most people who tried to kill ghosts ended up getting killed themselves. Bullets were no good against them. Silver daggers through the heart only worked on vampires. Ghosts didn't *have* hearts. The trick was to coax them to return to the grave. But how? She'd gone to a bookstore and read the back covers of the entire forty-book Bloodstains series, feeling the need to shower after to remove the gore splashing up from the artwork. None of the cases matched Helga's exactly. What would she report to Brooke and Tiffany at their meeting in the afternoon?

2.45. 3.02. Eyelids at half-mast, she railed in X-rated fashion against her insomnia, then sighed and picked up *Let Freedom Ring*. She considered bringing it down on her head, not caring if it broke her neck, but was too weak to lift the granite slab of a book high enough. She propped it on her chest, felt her ribs give, and grimly turned to Chapter Six. "While Britain's colonial policies…" she began. A moment later, it seemed, it was morning, the sun slapping her in the face.

Groaning, she closed her eyes against the glare. She felt dead, for an instant hoped she was, then recognized her room with disappointment. She fingered a strand of her blonde hair and endeavoured to focus her eyes upon it. She'd found grey hairs lately, necessitating search-and-destroy missions each morning. Groping for the hand mirror on her table, she held it up, squinted, then gasped. Half her hair had gone grey in the night.

She sat up, fully awake, her mind racing. She couldn't pull out all the grey hairs, unless she wanted to look half bald. If she got a buzz haircut, the silver would still show. She rejected wigs and shaving her head. She'd have to dye her hair. Not that she had any dye or the time to apply it. She'd pick some up on the way home from school. In the meantime, she resolved to wear her hair up and hidden beneath her floppy beret.

She crept to her door and listened, judging if the coast was clear to the bathroom. If her spiteful younger sister, a sophomore, got a look at her hair and blabbed, Danielle would have no course but suicide. She cracked the door, stuck out her nose, then dashed down the hall, her robe over her head. She locked the bathroom door behind her, turned on the shower, and sighed with relief. Then she slipped off her robe and nightgown, glanced down – and felt the blood halt in her veins.

"No!" she moaned and blinked her eyes, praying they were playing tricks from fatigue. Pushing her grandmotherly grey hair aside, she peered more closely at her breasts. Withered, wrinkled, pathetically droopy, they looked like they'd been deflated during the night. They now hung empty, pointing at the floor. The term "pickle tits" rose up in her mind, an epithet she'd once applied loudly and in mixed company to a rival, leading to the girl's eventual withdrawal from school and move out of state. Danielle's breasts not only hung low, they looked ancient, as if she'd exchanged them with some toothless crone from *National Geographic*. Never again, she vowed, would she shower in PE. She'd claim she had cramps and sit out the class. After a week of that, she'd excuse herself from showering on religious grounds. She'd forge a note from her minister, or some made-up Indian guru. She'd go to the Supreme Court if she must to keep her breasts from being seen!

She averted her eyes from them as she entered the shower and began to wash. She raged at Helga, begging God to smite her with acne, AIDS, cellulite. The list was cut short when she reached behind herself to wash her buttocks and found, in dismay, that they weren't where they used to be. She craned her neck, dropped her washcloth, and felt frantically with her hands. Aghast, she found them six inches lower than usual, sagging like a pair of flat tyres. She wavered, disbelieving, oblivious of her surroundings. She thought back to her taut, faultless figure, recalling her lengthy sessions beneath the outdoor shower at the beach, ostensibly to remove the sand, knowing the guys were stripping her in their minds. She closed her eyes, revolted by her body. Sinking down slowly, she sat on the tiles and let the water strike her head. She'd read horror novels by the score, had met demons, werewolves, and demented killers with blood on their hands and murder in their hearts. None of that, she swore, could touch the gruesome, ghastly terror of aging. She rested her head on her knees and cried.

Forty minutes later, she set out for school. She'd lost two more teeth at breakfast, but had been fortunate that both were molars. She reminded herself not to open her mouth wide. Sunglasses hid the dark bags below her eyes. Each strand of her hair had been pulled up and pinned tight, safe from sight beneath her red beret. She'd scooped her breasts into her jogging bra. She'd raised her posterior in similar fashion, squeezing it into her tightest lycra shorts. She wondered if others could sense the strain of wearing this clown's trunk of disguises or whether she looked perfectly normal. She crossed Via Serena, looked up, and ardently hoped for the latter answer. Drew was marching down his walk just at the moment she passed it.

"Hi," she said, delighted at her luck. She'd been trying to attract his attention for weeks, but could never find him without Helga at his side. "How ya doin'?" She flashed a big smile, then feared she'd revealed her missing teeth and quickly snapped her mouth shut.

"I'm late, as a matter of fact."

"Yeah?" She pushed the word out through her sealed lips. She glimpsed his BMW in the garage, between the Ferrari and the silver Rolls Royce. Labouring to match his long strides, she imagined riding with him in the Rolls, the envy of all the Huns. She wondered why he no longer drove, and why someone so rich would wear the same patched jeans and ratty shoes every day. Once they were a couple, she'd give his wardrobe a do-over.

"I usually leave at seven," he said.

Danielle pretended fascination with his words while stealthily checking her beret's position.

"Helga and I usually meet before school. To talk about what we've been reading."

Danielle strained to maintain her blithe expression. There'd been no trace of apology in his words, no remorse, no thought of her at all. For the first time, the fact struck her square between the eyes. He never *had* given her a thought. Though she saw him constantly in her mind, and saw herself as the love of his life and heir to his staggering fortune, he never noticed her at all unless, as today, she was blocking his path. Was he immune to good looks? Gay perhaps? Then why was he surgically attached to Helga? And before Helga there'd been Charity. Danielle's body outshone both of theirs, or had until that morning. She stared daggers at him from behind her dark glasses. Enraged at his rejection, clinging by her fingernails to her fantasies, she decided to lay her ace on the table.

"I suppose that you're aware," she stated, her voice trembling, "that Helga is a ghost." She waited smugly for her words to take effect.

"Right," said Drew.

They walked through the Hundred Palms Estates gateway.

"You think I'm kidding?" panted Danielle. She had a long coughing attack. She was having trouble keeping up and felt painfully short of breath.

"Kidding or crazy," Drew replied.

"I'm telling the truth!" shouted Danielle. "And I'm telling it for your own good!" She gazed at him, imploring him both to see her as his saviour and to stop so that she could catch her breath. Her appeals went unheard. He increased his speed seeming anxious to be rid of her.

"She's not real!" she cried. "There's no blood in

85

her body!" She withheld Helga's connection with Charity, fearing it might increase his devotion.

"Her body seemed warm-blooded enough when we were kissing last night."

Like a tranquillizing dart, the line halted-Danielle. Drew strode briskly onward.

"This is no joke!" she screamed at him. She took a few steps, then clung to a street sign, wheezing hoarsely. "I'm *serious!*"

"Try 'delirious'," Drew called back. He vanished around a corner.

Lungs aching, Danielle sat on the curb, inhaling deeply and sobbing. She was used to getting her own way and seethed at Drew for disregarding her grand plan. She now detested him as passionately as she'd loved him ten minutes before. She vowed he would pay for spurning her.

It was then that she remembered *Honeymoon in Hades* and realized it held the solution to all her problems.

CHAPTER THIRTEEN

Brooke grasped the wheelbarrow's wooden handles, lifted with a dramatic groan, and steered the mountain of compost towards the vegetable bed. It was late afternoon on Thursday. She'd made the same trip thirteen times and felt like a Chinese peasant from the pages of *The Good Earth*, which her class was reading in English. She resembled one, too, she reflected, in her baggy workshirt and big-brimmed straw hat. Plus her short stature, she reminded herself. She'd lost another half-inch that day. Only her Walkman and headphones, transmitting the latest release by Pus, placed her in present-day America.

She dumped her load beside the huge bed and squeezed the sweat from her face with her finger. Though the day was sweltering, her shirt's long sleeves were buttoned at the wrist to cover her liver spots. That morning she'd spied an ad in the paper for a cream that claimed to remove them. She'd clipped it out secretly in the bathroom, had used a false name, and had posted it with studied nonchalance before school. The address was in Puerto Rico. She wondered if she'd live to receive the product.

"First Daughter, you have visitors!"

Brooke started. She realized her mother was shouting. Between the music and her failing hearing, she wouldn't have noticed Godzilla approaching. She pulled out her headphones and listened to her mother repeat her announcement.

"May I go, Honoured Mother?" she asked.

She couldn't make out the soft-voiced answer, but had schooled herself in reading lips and thought that her mother had agreed. She washed her hands and face and found Danielle and Tiffany in the den.

"Incense – cool," said Tiffany.

Brooke let the comment pass, closed her nose against the hated scent, and led the way past her brother's room.

"What's going on in there?" asked Danielle. They listened to the low chanting from within.

"His tutor," said Brooke. "Teaching him prayers for the dead. Confucians are big on funeral rites."

"Could come in handy," Tiffany noted.

They reached Brooke's room, closed the door, and studied each other while making small talk. Suspiciously, Danielle eyed the red bandana on Tiffany's head. Brooke pondered Danielle's beret. Tiffany considered Danielle's sunglasses, an accessory she'd donned herself when she'd found, with a shriek, the wrinkles beside her eyes. She feigned scratching her wrist and glanced at her watch. Another four hours until the Lazarus 12-hour Wrinkle-Fighting Creme took full effect. She preferred to undergo this transformation, so lyrically described in the ad, in the privacy of her own room and felt anxious to be on her way.

"So what did you find out?" pressed Tiffany. "You know. In the horror books."

"Not much," said Danielle. "Except that getting rid of a ghost isn't easy. If you try to kill 'em, they usually just laugh and kill you instead. Then they come back in the sequel."

Danielle watched their faces fall. "Then, this morning," she continued, "I remembered *Honeymoon in Hades*."

The others leaned toward her as if magnetized.

"This boy and girl had got engaged in secret, on the first day of their senior year. They were going to get married right after graduation. But then he fell off the balcony of her apartment. Like thirty floors up. So then the girl, who's really hot, starts going out with all these other guys. And one by one they all get killed by the boyfriend's ghost. Wipes out half the football team." She paused for three deep, lung-dredging coughs. "The girlfriend tries to kill the boyfriend's ghost but can't. Then she realizes that he won't leave the earth till he gets what he wants – her. So *she* jumps off her balcony. Presto, the ghost disappears. He joins her in the underworld and everybody lives happily ever after."

Brooke cleaned out both her ears with a finger. "So what are we supposed to do?"

Danielle lowered her voice. "We kill Drew."

Silence reigned. Eyes expanded. Brooke's palms suddenly felt damp. Fearing they might be overheard, she closed all the windows, then stood on a chair and shut the heating vent.

"The only way to get rid of a ghost is to give it what it wants," whispered Danielle. "Charity wanted Drew, but we wouldn't let her have him. If we finally give him to her, she might forget about punishing us. She'll be happy at last. She can rest in peace. Just like in the book."

"What about Helga?" asked Tiffany.

"Helga *is* Charity. The minute Drew's dead, Helga will vanish, to be with him in the afterlife. I'm almost sure of it."

Brooke's face showed distaste. "I don't want to kill Drew."

"I'm not wild about it either," lied Danielle. After realizing she'd never possess him, she'd sworn that no other girl would either, or at least no other girl on earth. She smirked. Hadn't she warned him about Helga? And hadn't he rudely ridiculed her? Saving her own life by taking his would be sweet as clover honey.

"I don't know," murmured Tiffany.

"It's him or us!" said Danielle. She coughed again. "It's our only hope. Don't you understand that we're *dying*?" She tugged off her beret and pulled out her hairgrips. The others gasped. Her hair tumbled down. It was now entirely white.

"I skipped the nursing home this week because of my stupid breathing," she said. "And now this. I look like one of *them*!"

By way of comfort, Brooke raised her trouser leg. Her skin was cobwebbed with neon-purple varicose veins. She began to cry. Tiffany panicked, hoping she wouldn't be asked to ante up a matching revelation.

Danielle coughed again. "I swear I've got pneumonia or something." She cleared her throat. "She's *killing* us.

"Maybe it won't work. But ending Drew's life could save all three of ours. Maybe the aging will even reverse. We've got nothing to lose."

"But Drew does," said Brooke.

"He'll be *happier* there," Tiffany spoke up, casting her lot with Danielle. She began to pee into her nappy, an act she'd dreaded performing in public at first, but which she brought off now with perfect aplomb. "He'll be with the woman he loves. Forever." With Helga out of the picture, she wondered if she and Jonathan might be reunited as well. She recalled the last twenty times they'd made up – the tears, the euphoria, the reinstating of her special discount on all his merchandise. She prayed that Danielle's strategy would work.

Danielle faced Brooke. "What about you? Want to spend your birthday in an open coffin?" She eyed the liver spots on Brooke's forehead. "Or a closed coffin, for your sake."

Brooke closed her eyes. "I guess not."

"Then you're in?"

Brooke sighed. "If you're sure, I guess. That he'll be happy."

"Wouldn't you be?"

She swallowed. "I don't know. I've never had a boyfriend. Dead *or* alive." She began to cry.

"Trust me," said Danielle. "You'd be doing him a favour. He and Charity can have sex and discuss *War and Peace* for eternity."

Brooke wiped her eyes and nodded. The three stared at each other, sealing the scheme.

Tiffany leaned closer to the others. "Where do we do it?"

"At the park," said Danielle. "Where we met Charity. He should die exactly where she did. Just like in *Honeymoon in Hades*."

"When?" asked Tiffany. She hoped it was soon. If her cream didn't work, her wrinkles would reach past her sunglasses and she'd have no choice but to drop out of school and hide in her room.

"Two days?" said Danielle.

"Tomorrow," urged Tiffany.

"All right," she agreed. "Friday night."

Brooke exhaled. "What about Helga?"

"She'll be there. We want to make sure she sees the favour we're doing for her."

Tiffany nervously chewed her thumbnail. "And then there's, like, the question of how."

92

Danielle nodded. "Just leave that to me."

That night after dinner Danielle heard the *Serenity Cove* environmental tape rising up from the living room. She tiptoed down the stairs and saw her mother, eyes closed, reclining in a chair. Her father was stretched out on the floor. From the room's giant speakers came the soft slap of waves and the distant squawk of seagulls. Simultaneously, from a boombox, came some New Age piano music. Danielle wondered if this potent mixture was safe or whether a doctor's OK was needed. Could you die of a tranquillity overdose? It must have been a gruesome day at work.

She climbed the stairs and shut her door gently. She wouldn't have to worry about her parents overhearing. Her sister was conveniently out on a date. She picked up the telephone and dialled.

"Hello."

"Hi, Jonathan. It's Danielle."

"Oh, hi."

"Are you someplace where you can talk?"

"Yeah. I'm standing next to a phone."

"You know what I mean."

"I do?"

"Would you shut up and get serious."

"You called me just to tell me to shut up?"

Danielle sighed. "Actually, I called to ask if you wanted to make some money."

"I just got serious. How much?"

"It depends on what you charge."

"For what?"

Danielle lowered her voice. "You know how you drive out to Wilmington Heights and other places? To buy your *Playboys* and condoms and all that stuff in your special locker?"

"Yeah."

"And how you've got fake IDs to buy 'em with?"

"Yeah."

"And how people pay you extra for all the trouble you go to?"

"Yeah."

"Well, I'm willing to pay extra. I got some birthday money from my grandmother last month. Like four hundred dollars."

"What do you need? I'm having a special on condoms. Starting Tuesday, officially."

"That's not exactly what I had in mind."

"Don't tell me. An abortion. Sorry, I don't do 'em. I could sell you a coat hanger. Fifty-nine cents. Ten for five bucks." He chuckled. "Just kidding."

"*Well, I'm not.*"

"So what is it then?"

Danielle licked her lips. "I need ... a gun."

There was a long silence from Jonathan's end.

"For protection, right?"

"Exactly. Protection."

Another pause followed.

"I think I know where I can pick one up."

Danielle's face lit. "Yeah?"

"But I'll have to tack on a twenty per cent sur-

94

charge for high stress. Four hundred bucks should cover it."

"I need it tomorrow."

Jonathan considered. "The stores are closed already. I guess I could make a detour with the Meals on Wheels van in the morning. I'll tell the gun dealer I'm carrying a shipment of caviar and need armed protection."

"I don't care *what* you say," snapped Danielle. "Just have it for me after school."

"As long as you have the money for me *before* school. In cash."

"I'll have it. I'll be waiting by the gym."

Jonathan paused. "I can almost see your note to your grandmother now. 'Thank you so much for the birthday money. You'd be pleased to know that —'"

Danielle hung up.

CHAPTER FOURTEEN

At 8.15 on Friday evening three figures emerged slowly from a car parked beside Clifftop Park. Feeling their way through the dark, they reached the narrow asphalt path bordering the cliff and headed south. The fog had come in an hour before, heavy and wringing wet as laundry. The night air was chill, the park all but empty. The foghorn at Pelican Point called forlornly. Lit by the infrequent, fogdimmed streetlights, the group would have passed for a trio of widows. One was short and slightly humpbacked, one paused often to catch her breath, one used a cane and constantly shifted the conversation toward her arthritis.

"Damn this fog!" muttered Tiffany. "My stupid hip bones are killing me!"

"Be glad it rolled in," said Danielle. "Without it the park would be crawling with witnesses."

"If I get any gladder I'll *scream*." Tiffany stumbled and nearly made good her threat. She was

having some difficulty seeing, due to the inade-
quate lighting and her huge sunglasses – the sort
more often found on octogenarians. Although,
when combined with her cane, they gave the
impression that she was blind, they at least hid the
lengthening river systems of wrinkles emptying
into her eyes. The cream she'd applied with great
faith had failed. She'd tried three others, with similar results. Her hopes were now pinned solely on
murder.

"It was foggy that night with Charity," brooded
Brooke.

The foghorn gave two low blasts, as if agreeing
with her. The three passed under a streetlight,
watching their shadows grow from gnomes into
monsters.

"How could we ever kill someone named Charity?" Tiffany wondered aloud.

"Or someone as nice as Drew," added Brooke.

"Shut up!" hissed Danielle. The waves crashed
below. "We've already been all over that! It's too
late to change our minds now."

They walked in silence. Danielle felt her pocket
for the suicide note she'd composed for Drew.
She'd typed it at lunch in the computer lab. The
themes were the same ones she'd chosen for Charity's – devastating disappointment in love, indif-
ference to life, apologies to family – sprinkled with
Drew-specific details. She felt proud of the skilful
job she'd done and smugly fantasized about showing it to her raisin-faced English teacher, who'd

marked her last essay "Sloppy thinking and execution."

"Look!" whispered Brooke. "There he is!"

Danielle tore off her dark glasses, exposing the huge bags under her eyes. She made out the bench, then Drew on it. Alone.

"Perfect," she said. The invitation had worked. She'd typed it right after the suicide note, addressed it "My love" with some distaste, stressed the vital importance of the meeting, then typed, rather than signed, Helga's name. Then she'd printed it out in italics to give it a more feminine look.

"Remember," she coached the others, "we just happen to be here, too."

"Where's Helga?" asked Brooke.

"I put 8.45 on her invitation," explained Danielle. "If she'd got here before us, they might have taken off together." She turned to Tiffany. "You put it in her locker?"

"Through one of the vents. Number 1228."

Danielle looked about. No cops or drunks. She was pleased to note that the bench was partially screened by bushes and away from a streetlight. Less welcome was the sight of the waist-high fence tracing the cliff. It had been removed for repairs the night that Charity had fallen. It was now back in place, chain link instead of wood. They'd have to get Drew over it.

The three approached.

"Hey, that's Drew," spoke Danielle, pleasant

surprise in her voice.

Drew looked up, studied the wheezing, limping, spectacled figures before him, and wondered if the three witches had leapt from the copy of *Macbeth* in his pocket.

"Hi, Drew," said one of them.

"Tiffany?"

"Yeah."

He peered up at her. "What's with the cane?"

She shrugged. "I sort of twisted my ankle."

"And why the sunglasses? At night. In the fog. If I'm not prying."

She inhaled, rushing oxygen to the excuse-fabricating portion of her brain. "I had an eye test today? They tell you to wear dark glasses afterwards? To keep out the light for a while?"

He looked at Danielle. "You too?"

She nodded. "We both go to Dr Schlossburg," she lied.

Brooke edged forwards, feeling left out. "I go to him, too," she spoke up.

"Fascinating," Drew pronounced. "So what are you guys doing here?"

"Just walking," replied all three.

The sound of the waves rose up from below. Danielle scanned the distance for Helga.

"Not afraid of Jack the Ripper?" asked Drew.

Footsteps approached. Brooke clutched Danielle's arm, forgetting that they were the murderers. An old lady walking a dachshund emerged from the fog, stared at them in surprise, then continued into

99

invisibility. Her footsteps faded, then disappeared. A new set approached.

"Helga," said Drew.

She came near, in tight jeans and a white wool sweater, then recognized the Hun girls and stopped. Drew saw her face stiffen. He stood. "We'll see ya," he said to the Huns and took Helga's hand.

"Hold on," spoke Danielle. "The programme's hardly started. And we're the ones who arranged it, by putting those invitations in your lockers."

Drew and Helga stared at each other, then at Danielle.

"What is this?" said Drew.

"Just a little meeting." Danielle answered. She gave a long, rasping cough. "A chance for the truth to come out at last."

"And what truth is that?" Drew asked doubtfully.

A wave rammed into the rocks below. Danielle turned her gaze upon Helga. "That you're the ghost of Charity Chase. That we're here tonight to offer you Drew – if you'll spare our lives." She paused, then made up her mind to seek more. "And reverse what you've done to us."

The foghorn bayed. Brooke and Tiffany strained forward, faces taut, awaiting Helga's answer.

"What are you talking about?" demanded Drew.

"Ask Helga," Danielle replied.

"I don't understand," Helga stammered. "My school counsellor in Norway warned me that life here might seem strange for the first few months…" She broke off, at a loss for words. "Tell me! What is it I've done to you?"

Danielle snorted. "Don't waste our time. We *all* know exactly what you've done." Even though Drew would soon die, she was loath to list the catalogue of ills in his presence. If Helga did so, and mentioned Danielle's breasts, she'd jump off the cliff herself.

"And who," asked Helga, "is Charity Chase?"

Danielle sighed.

"The human you inhabited, *of course*," snapped Tiffany. "Before you came back to earth as a ghost."

Drew shook his head. "Not this again!"

"I'm *not* a ghost!" shouted Helga.

A jogger's loud footsteps, approaching the group, suddenly veered away at her words.

"Get real," said Danielle. "We know all about you. I've told Drew, too. There's no one to pretend for. As they say in Norway, 'the jig is up'."

Helga faced Drew. "What does this 'jig' mean? I don't know what they're talking about!"

"Sure you don't," Danielle said snidely. Her manner was that of a cop on the beat, wise to the ways of this world, and the next. "So tell us why you picked *this* bench to sit on whenever you came to the park. The same one Charity sat on before she died."

Helga eyed it in wonder. "*This* bench?" She seemed to scramble for words. "I never thought about it. Really. I suppose I like the view from here. But often I've sat on the other benches."

"Sound convincing?" Danielle addressed Drew, as if he were the jury.

He considered her point and glanced at Helga.

"And then there was your house," Danielle continued. "The school records showed you at two forty-four Gardenia Court. An address that *doesn't exist*."

Helga's brows writhed. "Two forty-four?"

"That's right."

"But I live at two *eighty*-four. The typist must have made a mistake. Perhaps because of the small amount of money you give to schools in this country, forcing the office to use volunteers."

Danielle smiled. "Ever hear of the term 'in denial'?" she said to Drew. "Have *you* ever actually been in her house?"

His eyes widening was his only reply.

"When we tried to cut your hair," Danielle went on, "you practically killed us all. Without ever laying a finger on us." She disallowed Helga's objection. "And then, after you promised there'd be justice, you said, 'That's why I've come'."

"It's true! That *is* why I've come. To learn about the American legal system. I hope to become a lawyer one day. That's why I've not reported you yet. I'm studying the laws of assault first, so that I can advise the dean."

"Knock off the acting," Danielle barked. "You came to get justice for Charity."

"Who is this Charity? Please answer me!"

"Which explains why you're killing us."

"I've done nothing!"

"Using your magical powers."

"It's all false!"

"Hidden in that telltale pale body."

"All Norwegians have fair skin!"

"That never sunburns."

"Or freckles," added Brooke.

"Because I put on sunscreen every day! As I absolutely must!"

"Which explains why you ditched biology when everyone had to prick their fingers. *There's not a drop of blood in your body!*"

"I have never ditched class! I had a dentist's appointment that could not be scheduled after school. I told the office and my teacher of this."

Danielle smiled in mock admiration. "And I thought I was the champion liar." She coughed, her lungs sounding waterlogged.

Helga faced Drew. "You believe me, don't you?"

Fog climbed over the cliff and coiled around them.

"She's a ghost!" warned Danielle. "They're experts at messing with mortals' minds. Don't be fooled!"

Drew studied Helga, indecision in his eyes. He

took up both her hands, and seemed to be judging them for warmth. "Let's talk it over," he said. "By ourselves."

The foghorn called. Drew and Helga started to leave.

"Not so fast." Danielle's voice quivered. "Like I said, you'll be joining Charity. In the format she'd want. As a spirit."

Drew turned. "What are you talking about?"

Danielle glanced around, then pulled from her jacket pocket the revolver that Jonathan had bought. She pointed it squarely at Drew. "Jump."

Tiffany gaped. Brooke covered her ears. Dumbstruck, dry-mouthed, Drew and Helga gawked in terror at Danielle.

"Drop her hand," she said.

Drew complied.

"Now climb over the fence and jump off. And join Charity, who wasn't a Hun. And who wasn't even *pretty*."

Drew struggled to make his tongue form words. "And what..." he babbled in a strange soprano, "what if I won't do it?"

Danielle had been afraid of this. She'd never fired a gun, and the soundtrack on the *Gun Safety* video she'd checked out from the library had been garbled, or perhaps was in Norwegian.

"Then I'll shoot you first, and *then* you'll go over." She tried to steady her wavering gun arm. "The suicide note I wrote leaves it open."

"Suicide note?"

104

"Just like Charity's."

Drew's disbelief surpassed itself. "*You* killed Charity?" he stuttered.

"We all did."

Brooke lowered her eyes.

Danielle caught the faint scuff of footsteps. "Jump!" she hissed.

Helga's head turned. She heard the footsteps, too.

"Yell and I'll shoot you, too," Danielle swore, forgetting that Helga was a ghost. She aimed at Drew's heart. *"Now!"* she ordered.

Drew backed up to the fence and raised one leg to the rail. He glanced at the dizzying 300-foot drop. Then, crouching low to minimize his target, he pushed off against the fence like a swimmer and dived at Danielle. At one and the same instant, a wave cracked like thunder on the rocks, the foghorn sounded, and Danielle's gun went off. The bullet rang against a metal fence post, then found flesh. Not Drew's, but Helga's.

Helga screamed. A man dashed up, saw Danielle in Drew's grasp on the ground, and expertly disarmed her. Helga clutched her wrist. Drew sprang up, rushed over to her, and pushed up her sweater's sleeve. Brooke and Tiffany clustered around her, staring in shock at Helga's wrist. A trickle of blood flowed from the wound.

The other girls' features froze at the sight. The foghorn moaned.

"Oops," said Tiffany.

CHAPTER FIFTEEN

Someone knocked on the open door.

"May I enter?" chirped a voice.

Danielle lay on the hospital bed, her wan, withered body limp as seaweed cast up on a rock. Laboriously, she lifted an eyelid. The white-haired woman who came into the room was unfamiliar.

"I believe I'll shut the door, if you don't mind, so that we can be alone." She did so, then surveyed Danielle's lodgings.

"A private room. How lucky you are. And everything so clean and modern." The woman's voice was soothing, her manner that of a doting grandmother. She put down her purse and a bag, then sat in the chair beside Danielle's bed.

"I read about you in the paper, of course." Her face took on a slightly stern cast. "I must say I'm glad that the off-duty policeman chanced to be walking his dog at that hour and halted matters before harm was done. But I've not come here to lecture you."

She viewed the plastic jungle of tubing supplying Danielle with food and medicines. On the bed's other side stood a respirator, which every few seconds pumped a breath into Danielle's lungs through a tube running to her mouth.

"You're plugged in all over, aren't you?" she said. "Pneumonia must be quite awful, I'm sure." The respirator sucked in air, then fed it into Danielle. Her chest rose. The visitor glanced at her hair, white at the roots, then becoming garishly blonde. Next she regarded Danielle's skin, pale and webbed with wrinkles like scalded milk. Though Danielle was not yet seventeen, she looked as old as a great-grandmother.

"My, how you've changed," she murmured softly. "But then, don't we all? Take me, for instance. Two months ago I had a stroke, couldn't talk, needed a walker – and now look at me."

Danielle attempted to do so, the motion of her eyes substituting for speech.

"Do you remember me, Danielle?" asked the woman. "I'm Mrs Witt. From the nursing home." She smiled. "I remember you."

Danielle, amazed, pushed her eyelids higher.

"I've just been to see the other girls. The doctors aren't sure yet whether they'll live."

Danielle's lips bunched briefly, contorted, then relaxed, unable to produce any words.

"But it's you whom I remember best."

She stood, looked over Danielle's get-well cards, then picked up a paperback entitled *Revenge of the Vampire Cheerleaders*.

"If it amuses you, I suppose." She shook her head, then put the book down. "Though I'm sad, I'll admit, that youngsters feel their lives so dull as to require such artificial shocks to keep them going. Ghosts and other such nonsense." She sighed. "Real life is so very dramatic just as it is, don't you think?"

She glanced at Danielle, then at some flowers in the room. "What could be more dramatic than death? Or more a part of life?" She inspected a cluster of carnations and broke off a wilted head.

"A friend of mine died just last month," she confided. "You met her at the nursing home. Estelle Beale. She was my roommate the first time that you came."

Danielle dimly recalled a red-wigged woman and the empty bed she'd left behind.

"We'd actually known each other for years. Our husbands were chemists at Cliffside Research. She suffered agonies waiting for death." Mrs Witt leaned down. "Then one day her husband gave her a shot of something that lifted her straightaway to heaven."

She raised the blinds and sampled Danielle's view.

"Death, however, is not always a blessing. Take Charity's, for instance." Her voice changed in texture. She turned towards Danielle. "Did you know

108

that she was my granddaughter?"

Mrs Witt's gaze bore into Danielle, whose blue eyes widened with comprehension.

"I thought not," the woman spoke for her. Her cheekbones shifted. She seemed to be pushing back tears. "Such a lovely child. So intelligent. And sweetnatured." She was silent, letting the words and their subject linger in the room a few moments.

"How she'd have loved your Community Service. She took pleasure in cheering people in need. As I was, when you were assigned to me." She sat down, pulled her chair close, and leaned forward, her face nearly touching Danielle's.

"You were right," she whispered. "I couldn't speak. Or write. But I could see. Quite well. And I saw how you were treating me." Her mouth became grim. "And I could hear. Which is how I found out that you and your friends were behind Charity's death."

Danielle's irises danced, the only sign of life in her sagging face. The respirator noisily inhaled.

"When I learned what you'd done, I asked Estelle's husband for an extra-large dose of his potion, in case I should ever need it myself. He brought it, along with a hypodermic needle. But it wasn't for me. It was for you. For you and your two friends."

Her voice was calm and matter-of-fact. She watched her words' effect in Danielle's agitated eyes.

"The potion was extremely concentrated, or so he said. You might be interested to know that it came from his work on aging agents. Something to do with chemical warfare. The dose was apparently large enough to handle all three of you, though slowly. The faster the heartbeat, the faster the aging accelerates, if I remember rightly."

Her thoughts whirling, Danielle recalled the near paralysis she and the others had suffered during the heart-quickening attempt to cut Helga's hair.

Mrs Witt leaned back in her chair, taking in Danielle's helplessness.

"I didn't tell your friends all this. Why, you might ask, am I telling you?" She paused, as if waiting for a reply. "There you have the answer. Your silence." She smiled. "You'll never speak again. Or write a word. Or take a step. My symptoms disappeared, as sometimes happens with strokes. You won't be so lucky." She leaned close to Danielle again. "The doctors have perhaps feared to tell you that you've only a day at most left to live."

Danielle's eyes darted wildly.

"Not that I'm so cruel as to wish you alone in your hour of need. Far from it. I'm here to be your companion. Just as you were mine."

With a grunt, she raised her heavy black shoes and brought them down upon Danielle's bed. Noticing that the TV was off, she took the remote, flicked it on, passed the music video station, and